PLAYERS

PLAYERS

Joyce Sweeney

WINSLOW PRESS

FLORIDA • NEW YORK

Acknowledgments:

I would like to thank the St. Gregory Crusaders: C.S. Sautter, Anthony Criscuolo,
Matt Mawhinney, Jamie Salmon, David Foster, Damian Sclafani, Casey Park,
and Brian Park. Thanks for letting me see firsthand the kind of team spirit I
wanted to write about. Also thanks to coaches Tom Donovan and Tom Hayes,
and especially to Sheila Portuando, a world class reading teacher.

Thanks also to my Thursday Group, who remind me every week
what it's like to be captain of a winning team.

As always, thanks to Jay, Heidi, and Joan for the usual good advice and moral support.

Thanks to George Nicholson for helping me find the right home for this book,
and to Francesca Crispino for her thoughtful and insightful editing.

Sweeney, Joyce.
Players / by Joyce Sweeney
First Edition
p.   cm.
Summary: Eighteen-year-old Corey sees a threat to his dream of winning
the basketball championship when he discovers that the new player on his team is a girl-stealing,
friend-framing, team-destroying force of evil.
ISBN 1-890817-54-6
[1. Basketball-Fiction.]
I. Title.
PZ7.S97427 Pl   2000
[Fic]–dc21
00-023329

10 9 8 7 6 5 4 3 2 1

*This book is dedicated to Cathy Lindstrandt
and Rosemary Jones. Both of you have taught me
that working quietly, tirelessly, and unselfishly
for the things you believe in can make
a huge difference in the world.*

Chapter

Even though Corey was supposed to be paying attention, he closed his eyes. He had never told anyone, not even Luke, about his discovery of "basketball music." Some things are just too personal and weird to say out loud.

He'd made the discovery his sophomore year, in a game against Douglas High. His ears had suddenly opened up, and  he realized there was a symphony going on around him—the thunking of the ball on the court, the rattle of the goal, twenty squeaking rubber soles, coaches screaming, kids cheering, players panting and grunting, refs whistling, buzzers buzzing. It was random, yet it meshed.

The only thing Corey could liken it to was the time his family went camping in the woods.

Just as he was falling asleep, the tree frogs and crickets seemed to grow louder, the wind rattled the palm fronds around him, he heard a distant brook. It all sounded strangely orchestrated.

Listening, Corey had discovered, could clear your mind, knock out the voices in your head that warn you your team is behind, time is running out, you haven't scored enough. Listening could put you back in your flow.

It was when Corey found this technique that he became the Badgers' high scorer, averaging thirty points a game with a personal best of fifty-one points. He and most of his squad made varsity their junior year, and St. Philip High School, never famous for basketball, suddenly had a team that was getting ink in all the local papers. They became the school to watch, and everyone said in their senior year they could go all-city. And now that year had arrived. Corey could practically smell the trophy.

There was just one problem. Robbie Sumlin, their big, beautiful, versatile, high-scoring center had been the only senior on the varsity first string. And now he had graduated—off to the University of Dayton. With Robbie gone, there was a hole in the first string that had to be flawlessly filled.

Corey opened his eyes again to view the frantic group of drilling, dribbling, shooting wannabes swirling over the court like a virus. There was some talent, of course, but really no one who could fill Robbie's size-sixteen shoes.

Corey elbowed Luke and whispered, "See anything?"

Luke was sitting in one of his profound slumps, arms folded so his letter jacket bunched up like a cocoon. "I see Coral Springs High getting our trophy," he growled.

Down on the floor, Coach Landis had already made a preliminary cut. He pulled out ten guys, instructed five to take off their shirts and set up a mock game. The boys who weren't chosen stood against the wall, muttering and glaring.

"There're a couple of new guys there," Corey said to Luke.

"Yeah," Luke said. "I see him."

Corey knew they were discussing the new kid, Noah somebody, curly red hair, freckles, maybe six feet three or six feet four, a dwarf next to Robbie, but aggressive and a good shooter. He had the ball now. Shirtless, he wove through his guards like a pale flame, put himself in perfect shooting position, then deliberately, he pivoted *away,* dribbled out to the three-point zone, and nailed it. He looked up at the bleachers where Corey and the rest of the varsity team were sitting and smiled.

Luke scowled. "A hot dog," he said. "You can lose games horsing around like that."

"You can win games with confidence like that," Corey said.

Luke fidgeted like he'd just realized he was sitting on something sharp. "There's something about him I don't like."

"What?" Corey said. "What do you see?"

Noah had just scored again. This time he caught Corey's eye directly and smiled again.

"For one thing, why does he keep looking up here?" Luke's feet hit the floor and he sat up straight. "It's bad etiquette. It's like…it's like the defendant staring at the jury." He pointed to a slender African-American guy. "What about this one?"

"He hasn't missed a shot," Corey agreed. "But he can't be more than five nine. And he's kind of passive, like, doesn't take the initiative."

"That could be control, Cor," Luke argued. "That could be poise."

"Poise!" Theo Stone, on Luke's other side, leaned into the discussion. He was their two-guard, a massive, muscular player with a deep, musical voice. "Poise!" he cried. "We judging these boys on poise? Antawn!" He grabbed Antawn Lewis by the shirt and literally pulled him into the discussion. "Throw out your notes. We supposed to be judging these boys on poise?"

Antawn was the point guard, the physical opposite of Theo. At five eleven he was considered small for basketball, but he was quick, flexible, and had the "jugular instinct."

"Poise!" he cackled. "What about the swimsuit competition? What about congeniality?"

Luke blushed. He was so blond, when he blushed it looked like he had a fever. "Screw you," he said mildly. "What are you guys ganging up on me for? Corey's the one trying to load the squad with white guys. He's pushing for that overgrown leprechaun down there!"

On the floor, Noah had scored again. The skins were murdering the shirts, mostly thanks to him. This time, as the ball dropped into the goal, he looked up at the bleachers and waved.

"He congenial, though," Antawn said.

***

Coach Landis needed a chalkboard to think. He wasn't supposed to be a coach, really, he was supposed to be a civics teacher; but somehow, the job had fallen to him. So he ran the team the way he knew how, like a civics class. He liked to pretend he was very democratic, which was why the varsity team had been judging tryouts. They were always discussing, debating, voting. Corey had noticed, however, that whenever the consensus went against something Landis really wanted, democracy was suspended.

All nine of them sat in front of the blackboard in two rows of chairs. The alternates, Ricky, Tim, Terelle, Joey, and Mike, had automatically lined up their chairs behind Corey, Luke, Theo, and Antawn. Another blow against democracy, Corey thought.

Landis fondled his whistle, an informal call to order.

"Okay, let's just start this by shouting out names to me. Who did you see out there who had potential?"

There were a couple of minutes of silence. Everyone on the squad, except Corey, was always reluctant to speak first. Corey called out, "Noah What's-his-name. The guy that was making all the triples."

"Trash," Luke muttered.

Landis laughed. "No, it's Travers. Noah Travers. Good pick, Corey. He's a transfer from Stone Mountain, Georgia. He was a center, a high scorer. I thought he was showing us some very good stuff today."

"Stone Mountain, Georgia?" Antawn cocked his head. "Did you say Stone Mountain, *Georgia*?"

"Don't go there." Landis was already greedily writing down Noah's name. "We don't judge people by where they come from."

"*You* don't!" Antawn said.

"I don't know his name," Luke said. "He was on the shirts team. Skinny, not real tall, bright blue shirt?"

"That's my second choice," Landis nodded. "Maurice Jones. A junior. He almost made the cut last year."

"Then he should have a shot over some transfer guy!" Luke said, looking directly at Corey. It was almost like they were having a fight.

"I saw him space out a couple of times," Corey said, looking at Landis, not at Luke. "He seemed like he had a concentration problem."

"Which is it?" Luke said. "Before you said he wasn't aggressive enough."

"It's kind of the same thing," Corey said.

"No, it's not."

They were glaring at each other.

"Let's just go with Maurice," Antawn said. "He's a brother and he's not from Georgia."

Landis, sensing he was losing control, touched his whistle again. "Come on, Antawn," he said. "That's not funny and it's not fair. If we put Noah on the team and there was any trouble with his attitude, you know I'd kick him off."

"It's just a factor," Antawn said. "That's all."

"And he's a jerk; that's another factor!" Luke said.

"How do you know that?" Corey raised his voice. "You don't even know him!"

Antawn giggled. "Uh-oh, Corey's in love!"

Everyone except Corey, who was busy cursing himself, erupted with laughter.

This time Landis raised the whistle off his chest a few inches. "Okay, okay, maybe I've got a solution you guys will like better. Take a look at this." He started drawing circles on the board—two rows of five.

"Great!" Antawn said. "We'll settle it with a game of tic-tac-toe!"

"Antawn, you're really talkative today," Landis said over his shoulder. Coming from him, this was a violent reprimand.

"Sorry."

"Okay, we're plugging a hole. Here's first string." Landis tapped the circles with his chalk. "Forward, forward, center, guard, guard. I think, since we have such an excellent first string, we should promote one of you guys to center."

"Luke," Corey said without hesitation.

"Okay," Landis said. "Why?"

"Well, none of us is really a center, so it's all equal that way. Luke's the tallest. Theo's second, but he's such a good guard, I wouldn't want to move him. I think Luke is the most aggressive of the four of us and the most flexible. He could do it."

"Antawn is way quicker than me," Luke said.

"I'm not tall enough," Antawn said. "And I'm too crazy."

This time the laughter was less tense. "You're not crazy," Landis said to Antawn. "But you can get overloaded and do reckless things. A center has to be really alert, but also really steady. I agree with Corey, that's Luke."

"Corey's the high scorer," Luke said. "What's wrong with him?"

Landis looked from Corey to Luke, apparently confused as to why they kept trying to pass this honor back and forth. "Corey, what do you say to that?"

"I'm not aggressive enough to play center," Corey said, which was the pure, painful truth.

Landis started putting names inside circles. "Let's make Luke the center; Corey stays our power forward, but we make him team captain? Because he is the high scorer, and Corey, I feel like you're a real emotional leader on this squad."

"Thank you," Corey said softly. He was stunned by the compliment and the murmurs of assent he heard around him.

"Now, if we move Antawn from point guard to small forward," Landis said, scribbling away happily, "we can get that craziness in motion and use it better. We all agree that Theo is a perfect guard; all we need is another good guard. So let's promote from within and bring Ricky up to first string."

Everyone cheered that. Ricky Lopez was a good guy, and a good shooter. Stunned by his promotion, he merely whispered, "Cool," as the team pounded on his back.

"You're a genius, man!" Antawn said. "You too good for a Catholic nowhere high school in Who-ever-heard-of-it, Florida. You should be a pro coach, man!"

"I know, but the scouts just haven't seen me," Landis said, grinning. "You guys will go all-city this year, and that's my ticket out of this dump. Now all we have to do is add one alternate. So the only question that remains is: Who should we take the chance on? Maurice or Noah? I'm gonna just go by a show of hands, but before you vote, I want you to really think. Who is best for the team? Not who do we like or where is the guy from or whether or not he's a brother, but which of those two guys played the best out there today? Okay, how many for Noah?"

Everyone raised their hand except Luke.

***

Corey could see Luke was deliberately hanging around after the meeting pretending to do things in his locker. Corey and Luke had lockers on opposite walls, and many times they had gotten through a difficult conversation by pretending to rearrange their stuff so they could speak back-to-back. Corey played along and transferred his shoes from the high shelf to the low shelf fourteen or fifteen times until the locker room was empty except for the two of them.

"We're okay, right?" Luke said.

"Sure. What else?"

Luke's voice carried some kind of urgency that Corey didn't understand. "We just have different opinions of this guy."

"No." Corey turned around and faced Luke's back. "I don't have an opinion yet and you do."

Luke slammed something. He was a hothead sometimes, you had to watch it.

"I'm right," Corey insisted gently. "You know he played the best. Everyone voted for him but you. What does that tell you?"

Luke swung around. His blue eyes weren't hostile, as Corey had expected, but sad looking. "It tells me that, once again, everybody else is wrong and I'm right." He smiled as if he were making a joke, but Corey thought he meant it.

Time to change the subject. "Well, anyway... congratulations on your undeserved promotion," Corey said.

Luke grinned. "And also with you." He hoisted his gym bag over his shoulder. "Claire's picking me up. Want a ride?" Claire was Luke's girlfriend, whom Corey secretly coveted. She played center for the girls' team and had long, long legs. She was as beautiful as a ballerina, brilliant, and didn't take herself seriously. Corey's girlfriend was a different type of person altogether. Corey smiled. "How much do you want me to say no?"

Luke laughed, and with that, Corey felt the final cords of tension between them break. "A lot!"

"I need the exercise," Corey said, stuffing things into his backpack. "I'm in no hurry to get home anyway, as you know." Corey's sister was getting married in a few weeks and the wedding had destroyed his happy family. "Tonight,

9

Beth's having all her friends over to figure out a bridesmaid dress that won't make them look fat."

"Yikes!" Luke hesitated at the doorway. "Well..."

"Yeah," said Corey, which officially ended their disagreement.

Luke smiled and ducked into the shadows.

Corey waited a decent interval so Luke and Claire could kiss and drive away in peace. Then he shouldered his backpack and headed out of the locker room, flipping off light switches as he went.

The back door behind the gym was always unlocked, and the foyer was left lit until ten. Corey thought of the many times he'd crossed the gym floor at night like this, when it was dark except for the slice of bright light from the foyer that made the edges of things look unnaturally sharp. The gym at night was magical, spiritual for him, a place where he thought about victories and analyzed losses, where he had built four years of trust with his teammates. In his dreams, he often went to the gym at night, where he might start out playing a game, and then while jumping up for a dunk, start levitating and flying around near the high ceiling, cheered on by the whole school. He stopped in the middle of the dark floor now, remembering, and slowly raised his arms.

"Corey." The voice was soft and close to his ear. Corey screamed involuntarily. Not a masculine yell, but a high-pitched schoolgirl scream. He'd always had a bad startle reaction. He turned in the half darkness, blood fizzing with adrenaline, and saw the angular silhouette of Noah Travers. "Jesus Christ!" Corey shouted. "You scared me!"

"I'm sorry." The voice was agreeable and pleasant, almost

sweet. Just a trace of a drawl. "I wanted to talk to you. I'm Noah Travers. I tried out for your team today." The silhouette extended its arm. *Your team?* Just an expression? Or did Noah know that Corey had just become the captain? Had he listened in on their meeting? Corey shook Noah's hand, trying to think. "I was wondering if I could talk to you."

"Sure, let's go out in the light where I can see you." Corey walked quickly through the dark gym, relieved to emerge into the brightly lit foyer, surrounded by dazzling trophy cases.

Noah walked more slowly, so Corey had to wait for him. His heart was still pounding. That was one of his main problems on the court, too. It took him too long to shake things off. When Noah finally stepped into the light, Corey said, "What are you doing here? You were supposed to go home after tryouts."

Up close, Noah was an Irish cliché: broad face, turned-up nose; even his eyes were green. There was something very open and friendly about him. Even now when he wasn't smiling, he gave the feeling that he was about to smile. "I wasn't eavesdropping," he said. "I was sitting in the bleachers. But I wanted to wait until everyone was gone and talk just to you."

How did you know I'd be the last to leave? "Okay, so what do you want?"

Noah was looking at the team photos and trophies. He spotted the one Corey got last year for his fifty-one-point game. "I got one of these back home. I was the high scorer for my school last year."

"Yeah, we…what do you want, Noah?"

"I'm sorry. You want to get home." Noah shifted his weight. "How do I say this? I want to make you understand. I just...Corey, I'm really good. Basketball is everything to me. I...I know everyone who tried out wants it, but I...I'm in a new school and basketball is everything to me."

Corey backed up a few steps. "We already voted, Noah, and the results will be posted out here on Monday. That's all I can say."

"No, no, I know that! I'm not trying to influence you, Corey. I was just hoping you could tell me something...give me some kind of hint, so I wouldn't have to go through the whole weekend...." He stepped forward a little, neatly compensating for the distance Corey had just created.

"I can't do that." Corey backed up some more. The door seemed kind of far away. "If we told one guy, we'd have to tell everyone. I mean, everyone who tried out will have a tough weekend...."

Noah was nodding rapidly. "I understand that. I guess I was hoping...that if you could see what it means to me, maybe you'd bend the rules a little."

"I can't. Why are you asking me? You're talking like you picked me out for some reason."

Noah smiled. "I guess I have a knack about people. I looked at all you guys sitting up there...boy what pressure that is! And I knew you were a good guy. I saw it in your face."

Note to self: Get new face. Corey felt behind him for the door bar. "I can't break the rules." His hand finally hit metal and he almost sighed with relief.

Noah took a huge step forward, almost a lunge. "I average,

like, twenty-five points a game."

Corey turned to open the door. "We had your stats. I really don't feel comfortable talking about it. Okay?" He pushed the door open and breathed in the night air.

"Does that mean?..." Noah's voice was at his ear again. *He can sure cover the floor fast.* A funny image appeared in Corey's head of crows and the way they move in leaps.

"I can't say anymore!" Corey made his voice loud and assertive and started half walking, half jogging across the parking lot.

Noah's voice called after him. "I've got my car. You want a ride?"

Corey broke into a run. "No!"

Chapter

Corey was a routine freak. He believed the edge in sports—
and maybe in everything—went to the people with healthy,
disciplined habits. He ran two miles, six days a week, and
practiced shooting every evening after dinner. Every
Saturday morning, his sister Renee went running with him.

Corey loved Renee. She was reliable, sensible, and
smart—his best friend in the family. Even
though she was only thirteen and Corey
was eighteen, he sometimes asked her
advice because it was usually on target.
He would never ask advice of his older
sister, Beth. She was like an alien to him.

But Renee. As he rolled out of bed and
slouched down the hall to the kitchen, he
could already picture her sitting in the
breakfast room waiting for him, her posture straight, sipping
herb tea, eating something healthy for breakfast, probably
reading something to improve his mind.

"What are you smiling at?" She looked up from
Smithsonian magazine. Her dark shiny hair cupped her chin
and lay in straight bangs across her forehead.

"Nothing." Corey cruised the kitchen, stopping at the
pantry and refrigerator, loading his arms with parts of his
breakfast: four slices of whole wheat bread, three eggs, the
orange juice carton, a tub of margarine.

"Who's Noah Travers?" Renee asked.

Corey dropped two eggs on the floor. "Huh?"

Renee adjusted her glasses. "Noah Travers. He just called."

Corey slowly pulled paper towels off the roll, wetting

them under the tap. "What did he say?"

She was back to her article. "He'll call back later."

Corey mopped up his mess, glancing at the clock on the stove. "He called at 7:30 in the morning? On a Saturday?"

She polished off her bran muffin and wiped her fingers on a napkin. "Yeah. He sounded nice. He asked me who I was and what grade I was in and stuff."

Corey felt little shakes at the backs of his knees. He suddenly wanted to change the subject. "How did the bridesmaid meeting end up last night?"

She laughed. "You mean after you and Mom and Dad all ran to your rooms? Oh, it was thrilling. One highlight for me was when Beth told me I was too young to be a bridesmaid and too old to be a flower girl, so the best thing would be for me to be nothing."

Corey beat his eggs into a froth, trying to shift his angry feelings from Noah to Beth. "She said it like that? She said you should be nothing?"

"Yeah, but then the attention focused on her friend Lindsay, who they all agreed was limiting the dress styles because she was such a 'big girl.'"

"Lindsay was right there when they said that?"

"Yes, blinking back her tears. Around that time, I suggested I could be an usher, like you."

Corey giggled. "I hope you timed that so Beth would choke on her Diet Pepsi."

Renee smiled. "Of course."

When Corey's eggs were done, he slid them onto a plate and pulled out a chair on the opposite side of the table from Renee. "I hope you never get married," he said.

Reading again, she smiled absently. "That makes two of us."

***

After running and taking a hot shower, Corey felt like a cat—muscles warm and stretched, ready to leap in any direction. He wondered if Luke would be around in the afternoon to shoot hoops.

This time the breakfast room was occupied by Beth, the blushing bride, who had finally risen from her royal bed. Her taffy-colored hair hung limply in her face, which was always puffy after sleep. Because she normally wore full makeup, she always looked startling without it—her eyes a size smaller, her cheeks pale and flat. She was hunched over a cup of coffee in her favorite flannel pajamas, picking polish off her nails. Corey fantasized about making a secret videotape of Beth in the morning to send to her fiancé, Don. But that would be a mistake. The objective was to get her out of the house. Corey had already surveyed her large, comfortable bedroom, mentally tearing down the rose-printed wallpaper, and hanging his NBA posters. "Where is everybody?" he asked.

"Renee went to Vicki's. Mom and Dad went to the mall." She yawned, flipping back her hair with one hand.

Once again, Corey prowled for food, this time assembling a lunch: more bread, a package of turkey from the deli, potato chips, a banana, a can of tomato soup.

"Who's Noah Travers?" Beth asked.

This time at least, he didn't drop anything. "This is like a bad dream!" he shouted.

Beth didn't respond. It was always safe to display emotion in front of her because she couldn't care less. "Did he leave a number?" Corey asked.

"No, he just said he'd call back. Who is he?"

Corey was feeling so agitated at this point, he was even willing to share his feelings with Beth. "He tried out for the team last night. He made it, but he doesn't know it. Last night he hung around the gym and tried to get me to tell him. Then he called this morning at 7:30 and talked to Renee, and now he's called again!"

Beth's eyes were glazed. "If he made the team, tell him."

"You don't do it that way. And Luke didn't like him...."

Her lip curled. "I don't think Luke is any great judge...."

"But now I'm starting to agree. He's kind of creepy, Beth. He's always smiling, and he asked Renee what grade she was in."

"That's good manners, Corey. Naturally, it would seem strange to you."

That's what you get. Frustrated, Corey took the offensive. "Where do you get off telling Renee she's not in the wedding?"

Beth shrugged. "I don't have a place for her."

Corey stacked his sandwich high and slathered it with mustard. "And your point about manners was what?"

"I'm only going to have one wedding!" Beth cried. She only had two tones of voice, sneering and wailing. "Can't I have it the way I want?"

"I don't know," Corey smiled. "We'll see what Mom says."

That drew blood. "You better butt out, you little creep, or

I'll put you in a kilt!"

"You do that and I'll flash your bridesmaids!"

She picked up her coffee. "The best thing about getting married," she hissed as she pushed past him, "is getting away from you!"

"I'll pass that along to Don!" Corey called.

Her bedroom door slammed in the distance.

Peace at last. Corey opened the tomato soup and heated it, stirring slowly to calm himself. His runner's tranquility was shattered. The kitchen phone seemed to be ticking.

Maybe he was being crazy. Maybe Noah was just an overeager, ridiculously polite guy. He hadn't really done anything. Beth, and more importantly Renee, hadn't reacted badly to him at all. Corey picked up the receiver and punched Luke's number.

"Hi, Captain!" The Zabinskis had Caller ID, so Luke always knew it was him.

"Hi. What are you doing?"

"Nothing. Want to come over?"

"Sure. You know what?"

"What?"

"Travers called me twice this morning."

"What'd he want?"

"I didn't talk to him. I think he wants to know if he made the team. He was waiting for me at the gym last night." Corey noticed the way those words rushed out of him.

"What do you mean?"

"He was sitting in the dark, in the gym, waiting for me to come out of the locker room so he could ask me if he made it. He kept saying how much basketball means to him."

"What a creep."

Corey hesitated, then said, "Maybe we should have all listened to you."

Luke coughed. "Too late for that now."

"No, I'm serious. This guy is giving me the creeps."

"See, this is what's wrong with you, Cor. First, everybody's Mother Theresa, then they're the anti-Christ. You've got to be more realistic."

"I'm a slow learner. But I'm asking you a serious question. I told him last night to wait until Monday. Then he calls my house twice this morning. What's that?"

"Corey, you wouldn't like my answer to that question."

"I'm asking."

Luke sighed loudly. "You're my best friend and I think you're great, Corey, but sometimes you can be a huge doormat. I don't think this guy is creepy. He's just pushy and you probably acted all wishy-washy last night, so he's pushing some more."

"Oh." Corey noticed his soup was boiling and turned off the burner.

"Don't be pissed off. You asked me."

"I know."

"Claire wants to know if you and Franny want to see *Death Comes Home* tonight."

"Ummm..." Corey wasn't sure what to say. Franny didn't like Luke or Claire and she'd told him absolutely to stop making dates with them. But Corey liked the idea of having all his favorite people together at once.

"Hello?" Luke called.

"Sorry."

"You in?"

Corey thought about that doormat comment. "Yeah. That would be great."

***

"You're in big trouble, mister," Franny hissed as they drove home. Her whole body was compressed with rage: knees squeezed together like a vise, arms folded tightly over her breasts. The message was very clear.

"Luke invited us and I didn't want to say no," Corey pleaded.

"Luke!" She made it sound like an expletive. "Do you know you just ran a yellow light? And who picked that movie? Is that the kind of movie you expect to get me in the mood with?"

The message was painfully clear. *Death Comes Home* had been a poor choice for a date movie, all about a battered woman running from her brutal, unfeeling husband. By the end of the first hour, Corey didn't like men himself. He'd tried to put his arm around Franny at one point and she'd looked at him like he was crazy. "We all wanted to see it. It got great reviews. I don't pick movies like a strategy to try and get you to—"

"That's obvious!"

Corey stopped at the next amber light and looked over at her. When he couldn't see her, like when they spoke on the phone, he often thought he didn't like her, but one glance, and he could fall right back into love again. She was a prize, the captain of the varsity cheerleaders, well-established as the most beautiful girl in the school. He let his eyes linger on her brown curls, her wide-set green eyes, her breasts, her perfect skin. People envied him for having her. It was worth making an effort to be her boyfriend. He could get hard right now at this traffic light just from looking at her.

Still, why did his mind wander to Claire? He saw a mental movie of Luke and Claire walking ahead of them into the theater: Claire tossing popcorn in Luke's hair, her blond ponytail a little too stringy, her face scrubbed and freckled, her outfit a study in grunge. But she was always smiling, relaxed, enjoying herself—not wound up like Franny always seemed to be.

Franny seemed to have been talking while his thoughts wandered. "And Pizza Hut! What am I supposed to eat at Pizza Hut? You know I'm on a diet."

"They have salads."

"I hate salads. All I ever eat are salads. The light is green, for your information!"

Corey hit the accelerator a little too hard and the car lurched forward. "Look, I'm sorry you didn't have a good time. Next weekend we'll do something you want to do."

"I might be busy next weekend." She patted the edges of her hair. "I don't know."

Right. "Luke's my friend, Franny. It would make me happy if—"

"Luke Zabinski is a jerk. He doesn't like me and he's stupid."

"No, he's not!" Corey couldn't watch the road and stay in love with her. It was too hard.

"When I mentioned Bill Gates, he had no idea who I was

talking about. He didn't have a clue!"

"That doesn't make him stupid. If he said something about Alonzo Mourning you wouldn't have a clue, would you?"

"And her! What's her problem? Is she a cross-dresser?"

"I think she's beautiful!" Corey shouted. He then resisted the impulse to smack himself in the head.

"Oh, you do, do you?"

Happily, they were at her house. "I'll try to do better," Corey grumbled. He waited for her to get out and slam the door, but she just sat there.

"I just get the feeling you care more about your friends than you do about me," she said in an alien-sounding meek voice. Corey looked over and saw that somehow she had gotten her eyes to brim with tears, making the lashes look wet and lovely. Corey knew he was being played, but wondered if he could still salvage some making out from the situation.

"I care about your feelings," he said.

She leaned forward a little. Corey picked up a waft of her jasmine cologne. Against his will, his gaze drifted down the front of her sweater. "I just want to feel special," she said. "Appreciated."

Now his hand was defying him, traveling up into her long brown curls. "You are special," he sighed.

Her lovely eyes opened wide. "You know what would be wonderful?"

"What?" Their faces were very close. He could smell her pepperminty breath.

"If we could go on a special date. Like a place where you'd dress up in a suit. Like La Vielle Maison or something."

Corey tried not to choke. Besides the idea of putting on a

suit on a Saturday night, there was the money he'd been saving up for a CD player all melting into a puddle of French sauces. "Well..."

Her clothing rustled as she scooted closer to him, artfully working around the gearshift. "If I felt really safe with you, really appreciated, I know I could relax more." She was whispering now, her fingers playing with the collar of his T-shirt. "Know what I mean?"

Yes. You're offering me sex in exchange for an expensive dinner you can tell your friends about. That was what the brain in his head was saying. The other one was screaming, *Go for it!* "I'll make a reservation," he sighed and leaned in for his reward kiss, which lasted fifteen minutes and left him sitting in her driveway for several more minutes after she'd gone into the house, throbbing and struggling to think about unsexy things so he could drive home safely. He fervently pictured his grandmother's funeral until all systems were quiet. "You are one lucky doormat," he muttered to himself.

***

When he walked into the house, the phone was ringing and he knew it was Noah. Beth jumped up and grabbed it—she always thought the phone was for her. "Hi, Noah!" she said. They were old friends by now, apparently. "Yes, he just walked in."

Corey was too emotionally exhausted to care. He walked past his family, who had been watching a documentary about monkeys, but had now turned to this more interesting drama. Corey wondered how many times Noah had called.

He took the cordless like a zombie. "Yeah."

"Corey, I've been trying to reach you all day."

Corey carried the phone toward his room, away from the family gaze. He stood in the dark hallway, leaning against the wall for support. "I know. What's your problem?"

A long hesitation at the other end. "I'm sorry. I'm being a pest."

Corey staggered into his room, not bothering to turn on a light. The darkness was soothing. He sat on the bed. "Yeah, kind of. I told you I wouldn't tell you anything. It's not fair to the other guys who tried out."

"I know." A deep sigh. "Okay, forget I called. I like...I'm not sleeping or anything is the problem. I didn't sleep last night. I keep going through every little move I made at tryouts, all the stupid mistakes I might have made—"

"You're on the team."

"What?"

"Get off my back. You made the team."

"Oh, my God! That's just great. Corey, thank you! Thank you so much!"

"Don't thank me, you earned it. I've had a really long day and I want to go to sleep now, okay?"

"Oh, sure, Corey, and thanks. I won't forget."

"You bet." Corey pushed the disconnect button hard. He slumped, still holding the phone. He didn't even bother to get undressed.

***

Corey dreamed he was playing basketball in a hospital. It

was an operating theater and doctors were working on a patient in the center of the court under one of those big, shiny lights. Instead of a scoreboard, there was a woman's voice, announcing every goal, *Visitors 30, Home 0, Visitors 32, Home 0.* Corey knew his team was the home team and they couldn't score. Every time they got near the goal there was a different obstacle. One time it was Franny, sitting in the net, blocking the shots. Another time, Corey tried to shoot and the whole backboard collapsed and melted into the floor. Another time, the goal ejected the ball, spat it right back out. Each time, the woman's voice would add two more points to the visitors' score.

Her voice was distracting, like the bright light over the operating table. Once, Corey bumped into the patient and the doctor shouted at him, "Don't you know someone could get killed?" Corey worried that the game was interfering with the operation. Still, he kept trying to score. Finally, he had a clear shot at the net: no guards around him and a perfect angle. He set himself, but just before he released, he felt someone grab him from behind, wrapping their arms around him like ropes.

"Hey!" Corey shouted. "I need to make a shot!" He twisted and saw it was Noah holding him.

"They need a heart!" Noah said, dragging Corey to the midline, toward the operating table. "You have to donate your heart!"

Corey went frantic, kicking and screaming, but Noah was strong and kept dragging him closer and closer to the surgeons. The doctors and nurses all looked up hopefully. "I won't do it! I won't do it!" Corey screamed. Then he heard the tone like you hear when a heart monitor goes dead, a long monotone. He hadn't heard it beeping before, but he knew it meant the patient had died.

"He's gone," someone said. The overhead light blinded Corey.

The scoreboard lady said, "Game over." Corey looked at the dead patient on the table. It was Luke.

He woke up crying. The moon was shining in his window, blinding him. The telephone receiver was still clutched in his hand. Somehow, he had failed to disconnect properly and the operator was saying over and over in the scoreboard lady's voice, "If you'd like to make a call…"

Chapter

Two forty-five. The clock was dragging and Mr. Hubbard was droning about existentialism, which sounded to Corey like a great philosophy to have if you wanted to spend your life in jail. In the back of the room, Antawn and Theo were both fidgeting. Corey was listening for it, plugged into their impatience. The first practice of the new season was fifteen

minutes away, and Corey felt like a rodeo bull trapped in one of those little gates, eager to charge.

"Mr. Brennan?" Mr. Hubbard was saying. It was the end of a question Corey hadn't heard at all. He cursed himself.

"Sir?" he said, trying to ignore the snickers from his loyal teammates at the back of the room.

Mr. Hubbard's eyes were narrowed. Corey had already identified him as an athlete-hater. "The significance of the desert in *The Stranger*, what possible symbolic reasons could Camus have had for choosing such a setting?"

Corey cleared his throat. English was his best subject. There was no reason to be afraid, even though he hadn't read the assignment and didn't know who Camus was. Keyword—the desert. "Maybe the main character was... thirsty for something?"

Mr. Hubbard's scraggly eyebrows lifted. "That's interesting, Mr. Brennan, very interesting. Not what I might have said, but right on target." He propped one hip on the edge of his desk. "What do you believe the protagonist was thirsty for?"

Just spin the wheel and take a shot. "Understanding?" He hadn't read a book in any English class yet where the hero wasn't misunderstood about something.

Hubbard clapped his hands. "Excellent, Mr. Brennan, excellent. I'm pleased to see you have other things on your mind besides the Badgers."

They always get a shot in, even when they're praising you, Corey thought. Meanwhile, behind him, Antawn, who knew Corey hadn't read the assignment, exhaled loudly, "Huh!"

"Mr. Lewis? Do you have something to add?" Mr. Hubbard asked.

"Oh, no!" Antawn said. "I was having trouble swallowing."

Two fifty-five. Corey wondered why he was so much more nervous than last year. Of course, this was the one that counted, but it was something else. He felt so...responsible. Had the title of team captain pressured him? He heard kids walking in the breezeway outside the classroom door. Some classes were over.

But Mr. Hubbard was on a roll now, sitting on his desk, waving his arms. "Aren't we all living in our own private deserts? Aren't we all thirsty for understanding?"

The bell rang and the class stampeded for the door, leaving Mr. Hubbard's question unanswered.

Luke, Claire, and Franny were already waiting outside, along with Antawn's girlfriend, Letitia. Theo didn't have a girlfriend.

"What took you so long?" Luke pulled at Corey's shirt to make him walk faster.

"Old Mother Hubbard was making a speech," Theo answered. "You see, Luke, Corey helped us all see that we live in a desert and we're all tiny grains of sand. Isn't that what you said, Corey?"

"No, no, no!" Antawn cried. "Corey said life is like a big litter box and the cat is always coming!"

Over the laughter, Corey said, "I said life is like a toilet and flush you!"

Franny had clamped onto Corey's arm. "I hate English," she said.

"I love English," Claire said and the two girls glared at each other as if it was a serious thing to fight about.

Holding her hate stare, Franny said to Claire, "Did I tell you Corey's taking me to La Vielle Maison on Saturday?"

Letitia smacked Antawn on the shoulder. "Oh! Now why can't you be like that?"

"Ow!" said Antawn. "Thank you, Corey!"

"Jeez, are you crazy?" Luke asked Corey. "You could go to Pizza Hut seven hundred times for what you'll spend at that place."

"Pizza Hut," Franny interjected, "is not to everyone's taste."

Before anyone could cut her down to size, the gym came into view and the whole group seemed to lose their train of thought. Noah was standing at the doorway, feet planted, hands formed into fists, aiming a look straight at Corey. It was a very intense look.

They had been walking in a loose couples formation, but now the girls fell back and the boys came forward. Corey particularly noticed that Luke had come up close, flanking him. "What's up?" Corey called out warily.

Noah raised a trembling finger to the squad roster posted on the wall. "You put me in second string!"

Corey could feel his own heartbeat. "That's right." He came to a stop several feet from Noah, halting the whole group.

"You told me I was going to play starting center."

Corey felt himself blush. Whenever he was accused of anything, true or false, he always felt guilty. "No, I told you you made the team." Suddenly, he didn't want to be captain anymore.

"I was starting center back home." Noah was holding his body so rigidly, it made him tremble.

"You ain't back home now," Antawn said quietly. "Now you here."

Noah never even looked at him. He shifted his hot green eyes in Luke's direction. "You ever play center before?"

"A little."

"I've played it a lot. I've played it all my life." Noah was almost spitting. "It's a hard position to play if you don't know what you're doing."

Corey was suddenly over his nerves. He took a deep breath and stepped forward. "We wouldn't have put Luke in that position if we weren't confident he could play it. We gave a lot of thought to that whole roster. This is the team you're on now and if you love basketball like you say you do, then you know you have to support the team and play your best wherever you are. You've got a very important job and we need to know we can count on you. Okay?" He heard supportive murmurs behind him.

Noah's eyes flicked around, taking readings on the whole

group in front of him. Then he went back to Corey. "You can't leave me on the bench. You have to tell me you'll put me in and let me show what I can do."

"I'm not Superman," Luke said. "What do you think, I'm going to play the whole game and have a heart attack just to hold you back? You'll get plenty of shots, you know that."

Noah's muscles relaxed and his body seemed to move backward, although his feet stayed planted. Something about his motions made Corey think of a snake. "Okay, we'll see what happens," he said and abruptly turned around and strolled toward the locker room.

Everyone else stayed back, catching their breath.

"This is the one we thought was so damn congenial," Theo said.

"It's like he's in a desert," Antawn said. "Thirsty for understanding."

"Let's drown him," Luke said flatly.

Corey barely listened to them. He was watching Franny, who had drifted to the doorway of the gym and was staring at Noah's receding form.

***

Even though everyone was itching to get out on the court and get moving, Landis had to haul out his chalkboard and give a speech about the importance of this season for all of them.

"Once in a while this happens," he said in a hushed voice. "At a school nobody expects, somehow a great team comes together and surprises all the experts. That's what you did last year, and now all the spotlights are going to be on you guys to see if you can do it again. When we play our opener next week you're going to see more reporters out there than you've ever seen before. You're going to have scouts and rumors of scouts...." He waited for a laugh, but didn't get it. "My point is, it's very exciting, but it's also going to be a pressure like you've never known before."

"I quit," said Antawn. Corey realized how important Antawn was, always joking when things got too tense.

Landis smiled. "This is what I want to say to you guys and I want you to try and remember it all season, no matter what happens. You're where you are today because of one reason and one reason only. You're a real team. I'm not saying there's not a lot of individual talent, but I think if you were scattered out at different schools, none of you would have done as well as you've done with each other. Now when it really counts, don't lose that. Don't start competing within the team or showing off. Don't beat yourself up if you make a mistake, it sets you up to make more. Noah, you're our only newcomer and you're going to discover this is a magic team. They're magic because of friendship, and now you're part of that. And before we even play one game, I just want you guys to know that whatever happens this season, you're the team I'm going to remember all my life as the best, no matter how long I coach here at St. Philip. Okay, let's go."

Corey stood up and almost stumbled. His eyes were full of tears.

**

They drilled for about a half hour, during which Corey observed that everyone seemed just a little off except Noah, who was flawless. Up in the bleachers, the girls' team sat, waiting their turn to get the court. Several feet away sat the cheerleaders. Occasionally, Claire and Franny would glare at each other across the distance.

Corey struggled to get in "flow" but his mind was too busy. He thought about what an important season it was, whether he would be scouted and offered any additional scholarships. He and Luke both had a free ticket to the University of Miami if they wanted it, which would mean they could play together another four years, but Corey knew if what his father would call a "better" school came along, he'd have to take it. What if he choked and made a complete fool of himself this season? Was Noah a serious problem? Was Luke going to cooperate, or take Noah on? Why did he have to go to a French restaurant this weekend? Was he competent to be a team captain?

Landis blew his whistle. "That's enough!" He gestured for the ball, the best way to get attention. "Let's do a mock game. Just to make it simple, first string against second string, so you can all play your correct positions. Luke, here's your goal, Noah, there's yours. Let's go for the tip-off." He jogged off to center court, dribbling along the way.

Bad idea, Corey thought, *making Luke and Noah into opponents right off the bat.* They would probably square off like a couple of tomcats. But Landis never worried about things like that.

Up went the ball, Luke got the tap, and sent it to Corey. *Think!* Corey set off for the goal, immediately confronted by

Noah popping up in front of him like a ghost in a fun house. *Where did you come from?* Corey dribbled around him while glancing at Antawn and Luke, feeling, or sensing, Noah circling behind him for another attack. In front of him and to the left, he also saw Tim White, who was supposed to be guarding him. Outmanned and not feeling his best, Corey located Ricky and passed. Ricky took a read on the goal and suddenly Noah was there in his face, crowding aggressively, but careful not to foul. Luke somehow charged between them, taking possession and making a shot even before Noah could react. But Noah was fast enough to get the ball and take off with it.

Running downcourt to catch him, Corey and Luke exchanged a look, *He's good.*

Antawn was the only man on the team fast enough to get ahead of Noah's drive and he was so wound up he circled too tightly and charged into Noah. Noah was either knocked off his feet, or wisely faked a fall. The whistle blew.

"Charging!" Landis said. "Antawn, you know better, if you'd held back a little, he'd have charged into you. Noah, take two shots. Noah and Luke, you both looked great. Corey, you're not with us."

Corey felt himself blush and glanced up at the bleachers, but Franny was busy talking to Letitia. They lined up for Noah's foul shots. Predictably, he was one of those preeners who took the whole ten seconds for each shot, showing off and perfecting his aim. They both went in.

Focused now by his anger at himself, Corey took the ball, dribbled all the way to the goal and scored, not even aware of who was around him. If only he could always play like that!

Noah took possession, apparently quite comfortable playing all five positions for his team, and dribbled off. This time, though, Theo was in his way, doing what he did best. His nickname was Stonehenge because he was like a wall. Nobody could get around him. Noah tried to pivot several ways, but saw the game was up and passed to Mike Bailey, who made the shot. Luke was under the basket and he and Corey passed it back and forth all the way downcourt, derailing Noah's strategy, since he couldn't tell which one of them to double-team. Finally, he made a definitive move toward Corey, who passed to Luke, who put it in.

"Six to four first string!" Landis called out, running along beside them. "Corey and Luke, good problem solving!"

Corey loved that but struggled to stay in the moment. Pride could throw you off as much as shame. The invincible Noah was on his way to the goal again. But this time, his independence cost him. All five of his opponents clustered on him, realizing Noah loved to run the show so much, he'd try not to pass—even to an open man.

It was true. Hemmed in by a human pentagon, Noah kept pivoting and looking, trying to edge forward, determined to fight this wall of resistance.

"Pass!" Landis screamed incredulously.

"No!" Noah shouted back. Miraculously, he had inched forward a little, pivoting and dodging the forest of arms in his face. Corey felt weird, almost like this was exciting for the wrong reasons. He felt like part of a mob whose goal was to hurt Noah.

Noah was panting like a bull, his freckled face a deep red and dripping sweat. Corey thought Landis should just stop the action at this point and tell them they were all being ridiculous, but for some reason, he didn't.

Something about Noah's body compressed suddenly, and Corey knew he was going to jump. Everyone did. Six bodies rose vertically in the air and it was beautiful for a second, until Corey realized Luke and Noah were going to collide. The crown of Noah's head smashed up under Luke's chin with a snapping sound, and the next thing was the ball going wild, straight into Corey's face, slamming the bridge of his nose and blinding him, as they all fell together in a mass of arms and legs.

The whistle seemed to be blowing a long, continuous note. "Get back, get apart, move back!" Landis was yelling as he rushed to them. "Let me see who's hurt."

Corey had landed on his hands and seat, his legs pinning Ricky's. They both untangled and scooted back, as did Antawn and Theo. The ones who didn't move were Luke, sprawled with his eyes open, and Noah, flat on his back with his eyes closed.

There was no blood, Corey was happy to see. He'd seen blood once in a game and never wanted to see it again. He'd been spooked for the next half-dozen games after that incident, not able to get close enough to anyone to be effective.

Landis went to Noah, who was clearly the worst off. "Luke, don't try to get up yet!" Landis knelt by Noah, cradling his head. "Somebody go in my office and get two ice packs."

Antawn sprinted off.

Luke was sitting up now, shaking his head to clear it. "He got me under the chin with his head, his forehead," he said to Landis. "I'm okay, just a bruise, I guess."

The girls arrived from the bleachers, most of them standing off to the side, but Claire knelt down beside Luke, and Franny stood over Landis, looking into Noah's face.

"I got hit with the ball," Corey said. "But I'm okay."

Antawn had just arrived with the ice packs. "Get one more for Corey," Landis handed one to Luke and held the other one against the visible knot on Noah's head. He pried open one of Noah's eyes and looked at it. "Where'd it get you Corey? Is anybody else hurt? We're going to the ER anyway, I want to check out anybody who has anything."

While the others answered no, Corey said, "Bridge of my nose. It's swelling." He looked at Franny, but she was still hovering over Noah, who was coming around now.

"Ow!" he said, trying to touch his head.

"You came up under Luke's jawbone," Landis said. "You remember?"

"Yeah."

"You see clearly? Anything blurred? You know who we are, what's going on?"

"Yeah, I'm okay, it just *hurts*." Noah looked up at Franny, who smiled.

Corey wondered if he was faking or exaggerating, and then wondered why he would even have such a nasty thought about a teammate.

"I guess you're both lucky you have such hard heads," Landis grumbled, and Corey realized that the coach was furious. When all these injuries were squared away, they were going to get a major lecture.

Antawn was back with Corey's ice. He held it up to his

face feeling like a bad child waiting for a scolding.

"You need an ambulance, Noah, or can we drive to the ER?" Landis asked him. "And please don't be a hero and get the school sued and me fired."

Noah laughed faintly and sat up to show his head was clear. "We can go in the car."

"I want to go, too!" Claire said.

"Me too," others echoed.

"Claire and Franny only—and you have to drive over yourselves. You guys know the ER doesn't like it when the whole team camps out in their waiting room. Nobody's going to die. You can wait till tomorrow for the story." Landis stood up and offered a hand to Noah.

Corey reached out for Luke. "I'll call all you guys tonight," he murmured. Hands slapped and patted at him and Luke.

"Make sure everything's locked up, Antawn!" Landis called. "We'll have another practice tomorrow night unless you hear otherwise because we obviously have a few fundamentals to discuss!"

Corey, Luke, and Noah waited outside for Landis to bring his car around to the gym door. Noah leaned against the building for support, clutching his ice pack with both hands. Corey touched his nose and wondered if he was going to look ugly. Then he prayed to all the Basketball Gods these injuries weren't going to affect the opening game Friday.

Corey noticed Luke making quick little glances at Noah. "Hey, I'm sorry," he said finally. "We were all crowding you and it probably drove you nuts."

Noah slowly swung his gaze to Luke. His green eyes

were as hard as river rocks. "It was good it happened, Zabinski. Now you know what I do with things that get in my way."

Chapter

Landis picked up his chalk, but didn't seem to have the energy to lift it to the board. "As I was saying yesterday," he sighed, "what makes you guys special is the way you work as a team."

Corey's head was so low his chin was pressing his collarbone. Team captain for a few days and the Badgers  had gone from smoking to choking. The physical damage from yesterday's skirmish was minor. Corey ended up with two black eyes. Noah had a bump on his head, but no concussion. The doctor told Luke he'd suffered something like whiplash and put him in a neck brace. There was some question whether he could play the opening game against St. Anthony on Friday.

The deeper damage, Corey knew, was to morale. Their secret weapon—cohesiveness—was shot. They no longer trusted each other, and obviously Landis had no faith in them either.

"I was thinking last night," he said, placing the chalk in its rail, "about which one of you guys I'd like to yell at the most."

Please not me, please, Jesus not me, Corey chanted silently.

"I think I want to start with you, Noah. I know you're the new guy, but you told us you knew so much about b-ball. It looked to me yesterday like you don't know anything at all. Or if you know it, you're too pigheaded to use it!"

Corey looked up. He'd never heard Landis that angry, not

even last season when Antawn mooned a reporter who was giving him bad copy.

Noah stared at Landis, his body rigid, his face red. Luke, on Noah's other side, was smiling.

Landis walked closer to Noah, forcing him to tilt his head back to maintain eye contact. "Let me tell you a real basic thing about basketball. The most important thing is the other team is NOT SUPPOSED TO KNOW WHAT YOU'RE GONNA DO!"

"I know that," Noah mumbled.

"You do? You do? Then tell me something. If you know that, how come all five of your opponents were able to swarm over you like a hive of bees?"

Noah finally dropped his gaze. "I wanted to make that shot."

Landis turned and walked away, pacing the floor like a lawyer now. "You wanted to make that shot. All you did, Noah, was make a foul that would have got your behind thrown out of a real game. You injured another player, you risked injury to yourself, you disrespected all your teammates because they were open and you wouldn't pass to them—all to make a shot you couldn't possibly make. Is there a strategy here I'm not seeing?"

His voice had gotten kind of high. Corey and Luke exchanged glances.

"You know, when it first happened, I thought maybe it was a strategy. Because I know you're smart and you won games back home. I thought, maybe you're luring them all to think you're so stupid you won't pass, and then you'd have four open men! That would have been a play, Noah.

But no, you really were that stupid!"

"Hey, look—" Noah said.

"I'm still talking!" Landis had circled around to stand over Noah again. Corey felt dizzy and realized he'd been holding his breath. "How am I supposed to have confidence in you? Sure I know you can shoot, but can you play with a team? How am I supposed to put you in if I think you'll pull stuff like this?"

Noah raised his voice. "Can I—"

"No! I want you to get this, Noah. I know you're not stupid. So I can't even tell myself that's the problem. All I can tell myself is that you smashed into Luke on purpose. The guy you might like to replace. You see where I'm going?"

"No, look, that's not it," Noah said, suddenly switching to a begging tone. "I just lost my temper. That's my problem. I don't want to hurt anybody."

"If you want to hurt people you can't play on this team."

"I don't...they were ganging up on me...I lost my temper. I've never done that in a real game. I swear. Please don't go by that. Give me a chance."

They locked eyes for several agonizing seconds.

"Please." Noah said. He turned to his teammates. "Please."

"I ought to leave it up to Luke," Landis said.

Luke looked off to the side. "Don't kick somebody off the team for me."

"All right," Landis said. "You got one more chance, Noah. Make the most of it."

Noah took a deep breath and let it out. "Thank you. Thank all of you."

"All right, just go out and drill today. I don't want to deal with any of you." Landis sat on his stool and turned away from them.

"Coach?" Noah asked.

"What is it?"

"Is Luke going to start on Friday, or do you want me to?"

Corey heard Antawn squeak with disbelief.

Landis closed his eyes. "I'm going talk that over with Corey."

No, no, no!

"Thank you." Noah took off.

Luke walked close to Corey as the rest of them filed out. "You better make the right decision, buddy," Luke muttered and then speeded up, walking to the bleachers without looking back. Corey vaguely heard Antawn's voice at his shoulder.

"Wouldn't want to be you!"

*****

Since Landis hadn't yelled at him, Corey spent the whole practice yelling at himself. To his mind, this was a failure for the team captain and no one else. Wasn't his job to keep the team cohesive? Landis's compliment, that Corey was an emotional leader, clanged around hollowly in his brain. He knew he wasn't leading, he was hanging back, letting Luke and Noah clash. He had to take some action, but what?

He looked up at the bleachers where Luke was lounging, surrounded by Claire and the girls' squad, glaring down at the guys who were allowed to practice.

Then Corey looked at Noah, standing in the rebound line, his back perfectly straight, frowning with concentration.

Like he expected the photographers at any moment. Did the guy ever stop auditioning?

Only one of them was going to start Friday and the other one was going to hate him.

Suddenly Corey knew what he should do. He needed to bring them together! That was the problem. They felt like enemies, not teammates. From the moment Luke lost the vote and Noah was put on the team, Corey should have been supporting Noah, helping Luke to accept him. Instead, Corey had been timid, trying too hard not to anger anyone.

Corey dropped out of the line and marched up into the bleachers.

Luke was leaning back against Claire. He looked a little hostile, but maybe it was just his neck brace forcing him to jut his chin out.

"Can I change seats with you?" Corey joked.

"We took a poll," Luke said. "They all think I should start Friday and not that punk."

The girls made affirmative noises.

"We'll see how your neck feels," Corey said. "I was thinking…"

"Uh-oh," Luke said.

His cheering section laughed. Corey noticed Franny was drifting over from Cheerleader Territory.

"Let's get a bunch of people and go someplace after practice," Corey said.

Luke was definitely sticking his chin out now. "Which people?"

Corey cleared his throat. "Whoever wants to go."

"That's a great idea," Claire said. "I'm in."

Corey could have kissed her.

Luke glanced at Claire, just a small warning, then turned back to Corey. "What if Noah wants to go?"

The girls' team had picked up on the tension and were watching Corey and Luke like a tennis audience. "Then he can go," Corey said.

"I'm out then," said Luke.

"Luke, stop it!" Claire pulled away from him. "This is bad for the team."

"It was bad for the team for him to try to break my neck!" Luke shouted.

Corey glanced nervously at the court, but no one seemed to have heard anything.

Franny put her hand on Luke's shoulder. "I think we should do it. You guys have to try to be friends."

Corey blinked at Franny. Had friendly aliens taken over her body? He turned back to Luke. "So, are you in?"

"Antawn and I will go," Letitia said.

"Oh?" Claire chided. "You speak for him?"

Letitia smiled. "Yes, I do!" The girls laughed.

"You're railroading me, Corey!" Luke said. "And you're using my own harem to do it!"

That was good. Any sign of humor was good. "Is it working?" Corey asked.

Luke snorted. "Hey. What do I care? You think you can have a tea party with me and that big Irish clown and that'll make everything all better, you go right ahead. But if he pulls out a gun and shoots me, you're going to feel really bad!"

"Not as bad as you would!" Corey said.

Everybody was laughing now. Then Luke got stiff again. "I'll go, but if he starts up with me, Cor, I'm not responsible."

Corey had already turned to go. He'd learned the minute you get a concession, you have to move out before you lose it. "Right."

"One more thing!" Luke called.

Corey stopped and turned.

"You look like a raccoon, man!" Luke smiled.

Corey had forgotten his eyes. He laughed. "Well, you look like John the Baptist!"

Luke was delighted. Any hint of blasphemy could always crack him up.

Corey went back to the team, smiling to himself. *Emotional leader.*

***

They ended up at the mall, because nobody could agree on where to eat. The group lost its cohesiveness right inside the door. Antawn spotted the arcade and slipped into the clanging, beeping shadows. Letitia and Franny only got as far as the Accessory Barn. That left Luke, Corey, Claire, and Noah shuffling toward the food court inside a roar of awkward silence.

"Let's get something to eat and talk seriously about the game plan for Friday," Corey said.

"I'm not hungry." Luke planted his feet and glared at Noah.

Noah immediately squared off. "Neither am I."

"Just get us some sodas," Claire said, taking Corey's sleeve. "Corey and I will get a table." She swirled Corey into a surge of fat ladies and stroller moms while Corey struggled not to get intoxicated from the smell of her shampoo. "I think it's great what you're doing," she whispered in his ear.

What he was doing right then was trying not to kiss her. He grabbed an empty table to break the spell. "We've got to get Luke and Noah working together," he said. "They're our best assets and I don't want them fighting each other."

Corey sat down and Claire pulled her chair close to his. Their knees bumped. She swept her hair up with one hand and dropped it down her back. There was a little cross hanging inside her shirt. Corey made mental photos of everything for later review. "Do you think Luke can start?" he asked her. "How much pain is he in? Because if he has to take a back seat on the opening game, that's a problem."

"I think he can do it," she said. "The doctor said it was his choice. I mean there's nothing dislocated or anything. And I think you're right. If Noah starts for him, his pride won't stand it."

As if on cue, both Corey and Claire glanced at the counter where Luke and Noah were buying sodas. It looked like they were fighting over who would have the privilege of paying. Noah was holding out money and Luke was shoving his hand back.

"But if we play him too soon and he's out for the season, he'll never get over it," Corey said. "I wish he would just chill out a little."

Claire leaned in even closer, making the whole room spin for Corey. "He thinks Noah hit him on purpose," she said. "And if you promise not to tell, I'll tell you a secret."

Her voice lowered to a whisper.

"Okay," Corey heard his voice crack.

"Luke is jealous."

Corey pulled back from her. "Of who? I mean, of what?"

She took his shirt and pulled him close again. She whispered right in his ear. "He thinks Noah's going to steal you away as a friend. He keeps saying how you defend Noah, you think he's wonderful...."

Corey was shocked. "That's crazy!"

"I know," she said. "But Luke is insecure in a lot of ways. Believe me. And don't tell him I told you that. He'd freak out!"

"No kidding. But what's his problem? I'm just trying to help Noah feel like he's one of us. Luke and I have been friends forever."

"It's just the way he is. I think because—" she broke off suddenly.

Corey looked up and saw Luke and Noah approaching, each holding one side of the tray like they were carrying a coffin. Apparently there had been a struggle over that, too.

"What are you doing sitting so close to my girlfriend?" Luke said, only half-humorously, Corey thought. He obediently moved his chair.

Luke took off his neck brace and set it on the table. "I really don't need this," he commented. He stretched and rotated his neck.

"Why don't you do a few pushups, Zabinski?" Noah asked.

"Why don't you—" Luke began.

Corey shoved his hand into the air between them. Not a threat, just a hand check. "All right! I'm fed up with you two!

I'm gonna tell you right now what I'm going to recommend for Friday and anybody who doesn't like it can fight with me, if you can find a place on my face that isn't bruised!"

To his surprise, they both faced front and gave him respectful looks.

Corey decided to exercise his power while he had it. "First, I just want to say that what you guys are doing really stinks. I know you both want that all-city as much as me and as much as Landis and as much as everybody on the team. What's between you two is not as important as that, am I right?"

"Right," Noah said.

"Whatever," said Luke.

"If you guys keep this crap up, you're going to blow it for all of us and that's not fair. I want you both to promise me that from now on you're going to think about the team and not your own stupid egos. Okay?"

"Okay, okay!" Luke said. "Who's starting?"

Corey took a deep breath. "I think Luke should start no matter how he feels because we don't want to start a buzz that our starting center is injured. That's what all the papers would write about if we gave them half a chance. I know you're not hurt that bad and even if you're faking me out a little, it's okay, you can hold out for at least one quarter so everything will look normal."

"Good!" said Luke.

"But," Corey said, "we'll put Noah in for the whole second, because you are injured and I want you to rest and assess yourself after you've played. Plus, again, it's good copy. We come in with a sub nobody's ever seen and if Noah shoots like we know he's capable, that will be a whole new buzz. Like, what's this secret weapon on our bench?"

"Yes!" Noah said.

Luke leaned across the table, sizing Corey up like a poker player. "What about the second half?"

"We'll decide at halftime. I want to see if you feel okay and just see how everything shakes down in the first. If you're okay, you can finish the whole game. I don't want to overexpose Noah the first time. You know? Just flash him and create a little stir. But we want to show a solid first string if we can."

"That makes sense," Luke said. He turned to Noah. "Don't you think?"

"I guess so," Noah said. "What if Luke's neck hurts? Then do I get to start the second?"

"It won't hurt!" Luke said.

"If it does," Corey said, "we aren't going to reinjure you and blow your whole season for you, obviously. Am I right?"

"Right," Luke said. "But it hardly hurts now. So don't get your little hopes up, Travers!"

Noah narrowed his eyes at Luke and turned back to Corey. "Thank you."

"Don't thank me, I'm just trying to have a decent strategy. And I don't know if Landis will go with any of this. And there is one more thing, Noah."

"What's that?"

"If you ever refuse to pass in a real game like you did in that practice, I will personally find a way to have your shorts *nailed* to the bench so you can never be in a game, because I like to keep my shooting average up, too, and I don't like people who don't share. Okay?"

Noah laughed. "Okay. Listen, both of you guys," he turned to Luke, "I'm sorry I got off on the wrong foot with you and with the team. I want to make all-city as much as you, and I swear I won't rock the boat. Okay?"

Corey said, "Okay."

Luke said, "We'll see."

***

As they walked out to their cars in the twilight, Corey began to realize he was late for dinner and would probably get yelled at. Still, he felt he'd made some progress.

Antawn had come out of the arcade pumped. Apparently he'd scored really well on a game called Exterminator, where you had to eliminate different household pests before they ate you. He was dancing around cars, singing a falsetto version of "History Repeating," while a mall security vehicle made slow circles around the area.

The girls walked together, Letitia and Franny including Claire for once, showing her all the earrings and scrunchies they'd bought.

Noah, Luke, and Corey—a cohesive group—walked out to Noah's car, discussing plays they might want to run. Noah had developed some plays back in Stone Mountain that were interesting. He drove off smiling and waving.

"Thanks." Luke clapped his hand around Corey's shoulder.

"For what?"

"You made it clear to that jerk that your first loyalty is to me. Now that he knows his place, maybe he'll behave."

Corey opened his mouth to correct the record, but

remembered what Claire had said and decided to leave well enough alone.

Letitia had caught up to Antawn at her car and scolded him for several seconds for horsing around. Then she smiled and he swung her around, pressing her against the car.

"Gives me ideas," Luke said. "See you." He trotted toward Claire.

Corey looked around for Franny just in time to see her car pull out of the lot.

Chapter

There was something about a game day. From the minute Corey opened his eyes Friday morning, something was humming in his bones. He knew the Badgers were going to do it this season. They were going to be unstoppable. He could feel the brass of the all-city trophy against his hands.

Ritualistically, he did everything perfectly throughout the day. He exercised perfectly, rested perfectly (during classes), ate his spaghetti two hours before gametime, avoided chocolate, visualized, rehearsed, remembered.

The team knew from last season to leave Corey alone the last hour before the game. In this final hour, Corey sat in front of his locker and thought about his own game, his personal strengths and weaknesses.

In the distance, he heard metal doors open and shut, toilets flushing, Antawn laughing as quietly as Antawn was capable. He saw guys walking back and forth in front of him, felt discreet pats on his shoulders, somehow registered the sight of Noah in a Badgers uniform for the first time, a Celtic warrior in red and black. He also remotely knew that Luke's neck was hurting him, "just a little," and there was a search underway for Tylenol.

But mostly, Corey thought about his game. All players, Corey believed, got one free gift from the Basketball Gods— one special talent they could always count on. Antawn was a psychic who knew which way other players were going to move. Theo could intimidate without fouling. Luke could strategize very fast, think on his feet. Corey's talent was that he could make perfect foul shots. Always. He couldn't remember the last time he'd missed a free throw in practice or a game. He couldn't see why it was hard for others.

Naturally that suggested a strategy. Landis had told him over and over to just go to the zone he wanted and let people foul him because it was a guaranteed two points.

The fly in the ointment was that Corey had trouble being aggressive. He knew he should charge fearlessly at those big guards, but he always wanted to shy back, pull away from all those elbows and hands. Sure, everyone had that reflex, but the rest of the team had mostly overcome it and Corey felt like a coward when he held back.

He and Landis had worked on it. Corey was supposed to think of the guards as paper cutouts, holograms, balloons. Corey was better than he used to be, as his averages showed, but sometimes the old fear would overtake him.

Now he was picturing himself as a bowling ball rolling into guard pins and suddenly he was aware of Noah sitting next to him.

"I'm sorry to bother you," Noah said.

Corey turned, annoyed. Noah was holding a Tylenol bottle between them, down and out of sight.

"Luke's neck is bothering him," Noah whispered. "They can't find any aspirin in the coach's office. Go give him this." He nudged the bottle into Corey's hand.

Corey looked through the open door into Landis's office where he and Luke were ransacking the place. Not good for Luke's game to be so riled up. "Why don't you give it to him?" Corey asked, still in a partial daze.

"Are you kidding? Luke doesn't trust me. He'd think I'm slipping him acid or something. Look, I just want us to win. I don't want our star center to miss a shot because he's in pain. You're the only person on the squad who'll believe me after what's happened. Please. Give it to him." He pushed the bottle into Corey's hand more forcefully. The pills rattled. Noah's green eyes looked concerned, almost sad. Corey thought about how hard it must be to come to a new school and play on a team where nobody really liked you. Noah had obviously picked up on that.

Corey took the bottle. "That's really nice of you. And don't feel bad. When Luke and the guys get to know you it won't be like this. You just got off on the wrong foot."

Noah smiled. "I'm not being nice, I'm being selfish. We screw up the opener, it could wreck the whole season."

"You're right." Corey stood up. "You're a good guy, Noah. I'll remember this." He went to the doorway of the office where Landis was now crawling on his hands and knees. Luke looked about one minute from exploding.

"Relax, boys!" Corey said. "The paramedics are here." He shook the bottle.

Luke rushed him and grabbed the Tylenol with both hands. "Oh, thank God! Where'd you get this? We didn't even bother you, the way you feel about pills."

Corey felt himself blush. "I was afraid you'd get a twinge so I came prepared, that's all."

Landis got a bottle of water out of the minicooler and offered it to Luke like an anxious mother. Luke shook out three caplets and washed them down with half the water. He looked at his watch. "I hope this has time to work!"

Corey turned Luke's wrist for a look. "Twenty minutes. You're home free." He held his hand up over Luke's head. "Peace be with you."

Luke exhaled deeply, finally relaxed. "And also with you. Thanks, pal."

***

For the next fifteen minutes, as the crowd-roar grew louder and louder on the other side of the locker room door, Landis, jumpy as a cat, tried to give them last minute instructions, punctuated by asking Luke every ten seconds how he felt.

Luke was unusually calm. "I don't even know I have a neck," he said at one point.

Confidence was soaring. The Badgers not only had Luke, they had Noah, a new mysterious element in their already powerful mix. They knew most of the St. Anthony squad, how to play them, what to do.

"I want to call you in and out, Antawn," Landis concluded. "You throw them off, we figured that out last year. I want them to get to the place where they don't know when you're going to pop up. Create as much confusion as you can."

"Pretend like you're in English class," Theo said to Antawn, pushing him affectionately.

"Remember how good you are," Landis said. "And keep your eyes off the cheerleaders and on the goal." They all put their hands together.

***

In religion class, Corey had always loved the stories of the Roman Coliseum. Of course, he understood the Romans were the bad guys, but still...the excitement of a little door opening somewhere and walking into an arena with thousands of people screaming all around you. Wow. It would be almost worth having a lion eat you or a gladiator stab you. All those people, looking at you.

Corey's favorite moment was this one—game time— when the locker room door opened and the Badgers came running out to warm up. When they were home, like now, a cheer went up from the crowd and you could listen for your own family or friends to call out your name. As they danced around, shooting and showing off, Corey watched three things—how well the Badgers were shooting (very), how well St. Anthony was shooting in their court (too good), and what the reporter from the *Sun-Sentinel* was doing. It was Patti Starr, who covered them last year. Corey liked her writing, but also felt sorry for her. She'd been a legendary power forward for UM's women's team years ago, before they had the WNBA, so after college, her only options were coaching and writing. It was sad. She was famous for the puns in her headlines, which sometimes could really hurt. One that stood out from a bad game last year was, BADGERS BITE.

When both teams had warmed up for about five minutes, they were called to their benches. St. Anthony didn't have a girls' team, so Claire's squad didn't get to play tonight. She had a seat in the front bleachers and was cupping her hands to her mouth, screaming Luke's name. Corey's heart began to race as they started setting time clocks. The referees began to confer, and the band and the cheerleaders moved into position. Corey twisted around and found his family, minus Beth. Renee went hysterical, screaming "Coreeeeee!" and waving both arms. Corey grinned and waved back. The band was playing "Tusk" (the music director was an ex-hippie), while the cheerleaders stepped and slid. Corey took a moment to contemplate Franny in her little black and red car wash skirt. She saw him and blew a kiss to the bench. Corey ducked his head.

Antawn's self-assigned job was psyching out and harassing the opposing bench. He always had an easy time with St. Anthony's because they were the Trojans. "Rubber heads!" he called, cupping his hands around his mouth. "We gonna stick a pin in you!"

Luke, next to Corey, had his medal out and held it in both hands, praying silently. Much as he liked to joke about religion, he really believed, while Corey did not. But then Luke had a cooler name-saint to pray to—a doctor, a gospel writer. Corey was named after some nut job whose only claim to fame was that he took a bite out of the same fish every day and never used it up. When Luke was finished, Corey put an arm around him. "Feel okay?"

Luke nodded. "Really good. Must have been extra strength. I haven't felt this good all week."

"Great." Corey gave him a squeeze and then thought how funny it was that it was okay for him to hug his teammates, hold hands with them, and slap their asses, but it wasn't cool to acknowledge a kiss from his girlfriend. It was a mixed-up world.

Claire came over to the bench, leaned over Luke and

gave him a kiss that Corey had to look away from. The band played a few strains of "Muskrat Love."

One minute to go. Landis swept along in back of the bench, embracing each player from behind, whispering personal advice. When he got to Corey he said, "Aggression."

Up in the stands, Renee was shrieking, "Corey Brennan is my brother!" The band wound down, the minute hand on the clock jumped. The scoreboard lights flashed on and the crowd got quieter. The Badgers clasped hands all down the line. The cheerleaders cleared the court. The referees stood up. Landis went over and shook hands with the Trojans' coach. The time clock flashed on. The buzzer sounded. The announcer blew into his microphone. Corey's mind went into chaos. Trojans were called individually to the court, to the weak cheers of their visiting fans. Antawn booed loudly until a referee looked at him. Corey looked at the big guy who was probably going to guard him. *Only a pack of cards,* he chanted in his head. *Only a pack of cards.*

He and Luke were squeezing hard. Corey noticed a tremor in Luke's hand.

"The Saint Philip High School Badgers!" called the announcer. Corey had to plug his ears against the screaming and air horns behind him.

"Playing forward, number 46, Team Captain Corey Brennan!" Corey jumped up and ran out, waving to the whole crowd, then to Renee exclusively.

"Playing forward, number 21, Antawn 'The Antagonist' Lewis!" Antawn ran out to Corey, high-fived, low-fived, and offered his hip, which made Corey double over laughing.

"Playing center, number 13, Luke 'The Physician'

Zabinski!" Luke jogged out, offered a hand to each of his forwards, smiled at Claire, and then turned a cold stare to the opposing center.

"Playing guard, number 7, Theo 'Stonehenge' Stone!" Theo walked out with his head down as if the cheering disturbed him. He offered the bleachers a shy nod.

"And finally, playing guard, number 15, Ricky 'The Wolf' Lopez!"

Corey had never had a nickname and envied the others. He wondered if there was something wrong with him, that no one ever gave him one. Of course you couldn't make a point of it or say anything, it had to happen naturally. But it bothered him, made him feel less like one of the guys.

"Ladies and gentlemen, St. Philip High School!" Screams, air horns. Corey watched Patti Starr, already talking into her tape recorder.

A referee carried the ball to center court. Luke and the other center stepped up, still glaring at each other. Luke raised his hand. Then he turned to Corey as if he wanted to say something and collapsed on the floor.

***

Sun-Sentinel
CENTER FOLDS—
BADGERS UNDAUNTED

St. Philip High School racked up their first victory last night in what is predicted to be one of the best seasons in the school's history, drop-kicking the St. Tony Trojans 71–43. The miracle is, they did it without their star player.

Luke Zabinski, the starting center, fainted on the court just prior to the tip-off, causing a twenty minute delay of the game while he was medically assessed. Although pronounced "fine" by coach Gregory Landis, the game went on without Zabinski, showcasing the considerable shooting talents of power forward Corey Brennan—40 points, and second-string phenom Noah Travers—25 points. Travers, a transfer student from Georgia, played so well (including five 3-point field goals), whispers of "ringer" swept the gym at the half.

"That's ridiculous," said Landis after the game. "If we thought Noah was a starter, we would have started him." Landis had nothing to say about the rumor that Zabinski had been injured earlier in the week and perhaps was not ready to start. "Luke is fine," Landis asserted. "We kept him out for the whole game to be cautious, but he was fine in the locker room. It was a fluke, but we like to play on the safe side with our players' health and welfare."

Meanwhile, Travers was a juggernaut, playing almost the entire game and never seeming to break a sweat. Whether the Trojans got a gift horse last night can never be proved, but here's the question for the teams scheduled to play St. Philip next—if they did this well without their star, what will they be like with him?

***

Corey read it five times, sifting it like a spin doctor before he picked up the phone and dialed Luke's number.

Luke answered, "What?!"

Corey lowered his voice to a meek level. "Just want to know how you feel today."

"How the hell do you think I feel?"

Corey paused, letting his body throw off that negative energy. "Did you see the paper?"

Luke groaned. "No. How bad is it?"

"It's good. She said, like, if we were this good without you, how good would we be with you?"

"She did not."

"Go read it. I swear to you."

"What does it say about Travers?"

"Well, obviously he got some ink. She raised some kind of ringer question but Landis told her what to do with that."

"Ringer! God, I hate him!"

"Don't say that... he's..."

"What does it say about...what happened to me?"

"It says you fainted, and she got from somewhere that you had an injury. But Landis made it clear you were good to go, no problem, you'd be in the next game...."

"What was in those pills you gave me?"

Corey was sitting at his kitchen table. Suddenly one of his legs started to shake. He looked at it in amazement. "You saw the bottle. It was Tylenol."

"Are you sure? I was so dizzy. Everything started spinning. I couldn't even see straight when the doctor was looking at me. Then today, bam, nothing, I feel fine."

Corey put his hand on the leg to stop it. "Did you eat dinner yesterday? Did you drink a lot of caffeine?"

"Caffeine my ass! I swear, if it wasn't you that gave me those Tylenol, I'd think—"

"A million things can make you faint. If you get up too fast you can faint."

"I took a Benadryl once and felt just like that, like my head was all empty and...echoing."

"Well, it can't be that because you took Tylenol. Did you ever have a problem with Tylenol?"

"No!"

"Then forget about it. It's a fluke. Things happen. Remember that time Theo threw up? Who knows what the body's doing?"

"Yeah..."

"I'll come over after I run...."

"Not today, Cor. I'm pretty down and I sure don't want you around trying to cheer me up. No offense."

Corey laughed. "None taken. You sure, though?"

"Yeah. Let me wallow in my pain. I'll call you tomorrow."

"Okay. Luke, you know you're my best friend, right?"

"Jeez, Corey! What, did the doctors tell you I'm gonna die or something?"

"I just...I'm always on your side, you know that."

"I thought there weren't supposed to be any sides."

"Yeah. But if there were...never mind, I'm babbling. I'd better go."

"Do you think? It sounds like any minute you're going to say, 'I love you, man.'"

"I love you, man," Corey said and quickly hung up.

He went to the bathroom and threw up his breakfast. Had he just lied? By not saying they were Noah's pills? If Luke knew that, he'd jump to the conclusion Noah poisoned him, and that would poison the team, the season, the championship.... But what if Noah had done something so awful? Did people ever do things like that in real life? That was in the movies. People didn't plot and do diabolical things.... But what if they did? Then Corey had just helped Noah, by covering it up.

Coming out of the bathroom, Corey met Beth in the hall. "Are you going to confession tonight?" he asked.

She had been trying to push past him, but she stopped dead, like he'd pulled a gun. "Yes, why?"

"Maybe I'll tag along," he said, then ran to his room before she could react.

***

After his run, Corey went over to the gym. He had a key to the locker room but not Landis's office. But the door was glass and you could see into the office.

Corey had a very good memory. After Luke took the pills, he'd put the bottle down on Landis's desk. Corey could play the tape in his head and see that. Then they went out and played the game. The bottle should still be there on the desk, because if Landis did anything with it, he would have given it back to Corey. It should still be there, forgotten in all the excitement. It wasn't.

Corey took a deep breath and went out to the hall to a pay phone.

Landis's wife answered, sleepy, sexy. "Hmmm?"

"Hello, Mrs. Landis. This is Corey Brennan."

"Oh, hi. Great game last night." Sheets rustled.

Corey struggled to focus on the task at hand. "Thank you.

Is Mr. Landis there?"

"Um-hmm. Here, sugar."

"Corey?"

"I'm sorry to bother you, sir."

"That's okay, no problem. We were out late last night, celebrating. Corey, I'm so impressed with you. You know what? I think you're the best shooter I've ever coached. I'm not kidding."

On any other day, that statement would have been a major event in Corey's life. But now it was just a distraction. "Thanks. You're a great coach. Wait till you see the paper. I called to ask you about something."

"Shoot."

"My Tylenol? That I gave Luke? Did you put it away in your desk?"

"Didn't you get it? We were looking for it last night."

"Huh?"

"When the doctor was checking Luke out in the locker room, he asked if Luke had had any medication, and then he wanted to see the Tylenol just to make sure you didn't accidentally give him something else. But we didn't see it and you were playing and it wasn't a big deal because Luke remembered for sure it was Tylenol and we just figured you had picked it up and put it back in your locker."

"Oh."

"Is it missing? I'll buy you another bottle."

"Oh, no, it's not a big deal. It's just—"

"Luke was fine by the half if you're worried. I just didn't want to fool around with it. But he was fine. I could've put him in. I think he just got overexcited."

Corey closed his eyes. "Yeah," he whispered.

"Anything else?" Landis was sounding impatient.

"No. I'll see you Monday." Corey hung up.

Who would take it away but Noah? And why? Because he put something that looked like Tylenol in the Tylenol bottle. And he used Corey, like a fool, to poison his own best friend before a game. Maybe. What happened if you accused somebody of something terrible and you were wrong? What happened if you knew somebody was really dangerous and you didn't do anything about it? Corey stood for a long time, feeling every ache and pain from the game last night in all his muscles and joints. Then he fed some more change into the phone and dialed Noah's number.

Chapter

Noah answered on the first ring. "Hello?"

"Hi, it's me. Nice work last night."

Noah's voice had an edge when he answered but now it zoomed into high gear. "Did you see the paper?"

"Yeah."

"Wow!"

"Yeah. Wow. Listen, Luke's gonna be okay. Nobody knows what it was, but he's fine."

"Oh, good. I was really worried. I mean it worked out great for me, but—"

"Yeah, listen. You doing anything right now?"

"Me? No. Why?"

"You want to do something? Hang out? Practice shooting?"

"*Sure.* Just let me—"

"I'll come over there. You're right off Westview, right?"

"Yeah, but—"

"Fifteen minutes? Unless you don't want to."

"No! No! I...I'll see you then."

"Good."

Corey felt better now. He was taking control. He knew he could look Noah in the eye and ask a few choice questions and definitely be able to tell what was what. Then he'd know what to do.

Since he was on a roll, he decided to reward himself with a call to Franny.

"Hello?" Sleepy, maybe still in bed.

"What have you got on?"

She giggled. "None of your business. But I can tell you, it's not very much...."

Corey shifted his already humming body and growled, "Don't move. I'll be right over."

"Corey, you were incredible last night."

"We didn't even have a date—oh! You mean the basketball game!"

She laughed. "The way you put that ball through the hoop...."

"Excuse me," Corey said. "I have to go now."

"And Noah. Isn't he something?"

The humming slowed down. "He's something all right. Don't you want to ask how Luke is?"

"They said he was okay last night. I think it was divine intervention. Noah should have started in the first place."

"Let's make a deal, Frances. I don't tell you which of your girls should stand on top of the pyramid, and you don't tell me who should start in my games."

She sniffed. "I just think Noah's a better player than Luke."

"He's not!" Corey stood up straighter, all humming at a dead stop. "I'm not as good as Luke and Noah's not as good as me!"

"Well, all I know is, Lorenzo Mourning doesn't faint before a game."

"Alonzo Mourning, Franny. Alonzo Mourning."

"Whatever. Did you talk to Luke? He must be so embarrassed."

"Let's get back to the purpose of my call," Corey said. "I have tons of other friends to talk about games with."

She giggled. "And the purpose of your call was?..."

"Well, I don't look like a raccoon anymore, so I was wondering if I am fit to take milady out to that French restaurant tonight, as requested."

"Oh, not tonight."

Corey listened to the static on the line. "What do you mean? It's Saturday."

"I've got something I have to do."

"When were you going to tell me that? You and me have gone out every Saturday night since last spring."

"You're exaggerating. I can't help it if something comes up."

Corey struggled not to raise his voice. "What came up?"

"It's a family thing. Too boring to go into. What? I'm sorry, my mom is screaming at me. I've gotta go."

"What kind of family thing? Contesting a will? Donating vital organs?"

"Corey, come on, you're—All RIGHT, Mother! I've really gotta go. I'll see you Monday."

The phone went dead, but Corey wasn't done. "What do you mean Monday?" he shouted at the receiver. "You can't call me tomorrow?"

All he got was a dial tone.

***

Corey got to Noah's around eleven. It was a big place, what the real estate ads would call an executive home, on a golf course. Before Corey could even ring the bell, Noah opened the door a sliver, holding onto it, like Corey was a salesman who might put his foot in the door. He looked bad. He hadn't shaved and had reddish stubble on his cheeks and chin. His eyes were puffy. "Hi, Corey."

"Hi. Can I—"

"Could we maybe go to your house?" Noah was bouncing on the balls of his feet.

"I just rode my bike all the way up here!"

"I know but can we just put it in my car? See, my mother isn't feeling well—"

"NOAH!" A shout came from inside the house. "What's going on? Who are you talking to?"

It was a woman's voice, but it was so harsh and raw it made Corey instinctively step back from the door.

Noah grimaced and screamed over his shoulder. "It's a friend of mine. I'm going out for a little while!"

"The hell you are! Don't you dare go anywhere! Do you think you can leave me?..."

Noah came all the way out, closing the door on her shrill voice. "Let's just go, okay?" he said to Corey.

Corey stared at the door, which still rang with muffled curses. "Are you sure it's okay?"

Noah was already walking to his car, head down, his ears bright red. "It's better if I go. She'll go back to sleep." He stood by his black Nissan and held the passenger door open for Corey. "Please. Let's get out of here."

Corey went to get his bike. He remembered Noah telling him the first day they met how much basketball meant to him. *It's all I have.* Now Corey understood what that meant.

***.

They ate a silent, completely awkward lunch at Star Burger. That is, Noah ate and Corey drank a carton of orange juice and a carton of milk, the only items on the menu he was willing to put in his body. Three times, Corey opened his mouth to ask Noah about his mother and three times, he closed it. On the fourth try, he got one word out. "Alcohol?"

Noah had been stuffing his mouth at top speed. He froze now and stared at Corey. Then he slowly put down the burger in his left hand and the fries in his right. He chewed and swallowed. "No. Pills."

Pills?

"She's been an addict since my dad died. Painkillers. She's fond of saying, 'There're all kinds of pain.' She's got about five new doctors lined up here in town already. She always likes to have a network of sources."

"When did your dad die? Do you mind me asking you this stuff?"

"No, I guess not. Nobody's ever bothered to ask me anything before. I guess this is something friends do, huh?"

Corey felt a small wave of shame, since he was actually trying to interrogate the guy. "Yeah," he mumbled.

"Eight years ago. I was ten."

"What did he die of?"

Noah coughed. "Suicide."

"Oh! Oh, God, I'm sorry!"

"It's okay, you didn't know. You expected me to say heart attack or something like that. But not me!" Noah forced a smile. "I have to be different."

Corey almost wanted to give him a little pat on the arm or something, but obviously, that would be a bad idea. "You the only child?"

"Yeah. But enough about me. Okay? Let's talk about the game. Wow! You're a great shooter. Almost as good as me."

"I'm better than you, Noah. And don't you ever forget it. But...it sure was weird about Luke, wasn't it?"

Noah sucked his Coke straw. "Yeah. Weird. He ever do anything like that before?"

"No! He's as strong as an ox."

"Could have even been a mental block, you know? From the anxiety. Some people, when they're really under pressure—"

"Not Luke. He's the coolest one on the team."

"But this season is different. It might be too much for him."

Corey looked straight into Noah's eyes. "Is that what you're hoping for?"

Noah slapped the table with both hands. "Stop that! When is everyone going to stop ragging on me about that? I mean, you should be thanking me for subbing so well, not—"

"Noah, look at me. Was that really Tylenol you gave me to give him?"

Noah's eyes widened. "Oh, my God. Is that what you think?"

"I don't know you well enough to think anything. That's why I'm asking you."

Noah rubbed his forehead. "Oh, now I get it. My mom's a junkie, so I have pills all over the house. And I'm so evil and diabolical that I'll slip drugs to a teammate so I can be the star. Is that the story?"

Corey felt hot and shaky, but he tried to look steady. "You

tell me."

Noah sat back in his chair. He took a deep breath and let it out. "Okay, I guess you don't know me. And you love your buddy, so if he messes up, it has to be the boogeyman, right? How can I make you believe I didn't do it?"

"Just say, 'I didn't do it.'"

"I didn't! I wouldn't! I wouldn't even think of something like that! I was trying to help Luke last night! Corey—the whole reason I love sports is…it's really all about honor. I grew up… My mom and dad both… You see the house I live in? We've got a fortune because my dad swindled and sued innocent people through his whole career. He probably killed himself because he was about to get caught at something!"

People were looking at them. "Noah, lower your voice."

"No! I'm on trial! I can see that! After he died and left us his dirty money, that still wasn't enough for Mom. She's collecting all kinds of disability and stuff, just to support her wardrobe and her pill habit!"

Corey could hardly stand to hear a guy talk this way about his mother, even if it was true. He put his hand up. "Noah, stop."

"No! I'm not finished. Basketball saved me. I learned from my coaches there are things in this world like honor and pride…. I love the trophies I have because they're earned. They're mine because I earned them!" He pounded his heart. "My mom gets her money and attention and everything else she wants by cheating. But…even if it kills me, I'm going to be different. And when someone like you comes along and—"

"Okay." Corey was drenched in sweat, just from listening.

"I get it."

"You believe me? It's really important. I don't care what the other guys think of me, but I need to know you're behind me, Corey. I know the black guys don't trust me because of where I'm from. You're my only friend on the team. Please."

"Okay, Noah. I believe you."

"If you suspect a lot of stuff and tell people, they'll use it! They'll railroad me right off the squad! You know?" Noah's knuckles were white, gripping the edge of the table.

"What did I just say? I didn't know a lot about you before. Now I do. Let's just forget it. Let's go to my house and shoot some hoops. I'm sorry if I upset you."

"I just want a fair chance, Corey. A fair chance to show you and Landis and everybody what I can do."

"Okay." Corey stood up. "Let's get out of here." He threw his cartons in the trash. Some of the people in the restaurant were still staring when they walked out the door.

Case closed, Corey thought to himself. *Nobody could show that kind of feeling if they were lying. Maybe Luke does have a problem with pressure.*

***

They played one-on-one, at which they were very evenly matched. Corey was the better shooter, but Noah could make up the difference by being more aggressive. Halfway through the game, a very odd event occurred. Renee, who spent every Saturday afternoon either glued to her computer or glued to a friend's computer, came out of the house, set up a deck chair and watched them play. Corey had played basketball with Luke in this driveway maybe thousands of times, but she'd never come out to watch them. Something about her looked different, too. Corey wondered if she'd put makeup on.

When Corey finally won the game, by the narrowest of margins, he threw Noah a car wash towel, got one for himself, and they headed for the shady spot in front of the house, where Renee was camped.

"Would you guys like a cold drink?" she asked, jumping up. "You really played hard."

Corey, who had burned up his last calorie hours ago and was sure his metabolism was now grinding up his bones for nourishment, croaked, "Orange juice. Just bring the jug."

"You have Gatorade?" Noah asked her. He stuck out his hand. "Hi, I'm Noah, Corey's friend. We talked on the phone once."

"I remember," she said. "I saw you at the game last night. You were terrific. I'm Corey's sister, Renee."

"Well, hi, Renee, it's nice to meet you."

"We have pink Gatorade and green Gatorade," she said, still holding his hand.

Noah smiled and gently pulled it away. "Green, please."

"You got it." She bounced into the house.

"Pretty," Noah commented.

"Thirteen," Corey said.

"I hear you!" Noah said. "I didn't mean it like that, anyway."

"She's got a crush on you, I think," Corey said. "So be nice. But not too nice."

"Don't worry. You know who I think has a crush on you?"

Corey was still sweating. He wiped his face off again. "Who?"

Noah grinned tauntingly. "Claire."

Corey wondered if his trembling was fear or hunger. "No..."

"Yes! I saw the way she pulled you off to a table by yourselves at the mall. And she was leaning into you, practically sitting in your lap, brushing little hairs out of your face... I've seen it all before, buddy. She was making a move."

The phone rang inside the house. Corey wondered if it was Franny reconsidering about tonight. "Quit it," he said to Noah. "That's not even good as a joke. She's Luke's girlfriend. She loves him. And she didn't brush little hairs out of my eyes."

Noah chuckled. "You just don't notice because you've got yourself something better. But that girl likes you, man. I've got radar about these things."

Corey's heart was pounding. If he ever thought Claire liked him back, he wouldn't know what to do. It would destroy his friendship with Luke. But on the other hand...Claire... "Turn your radar off," Corey muttered. "It's making an annoying noise."

"Fair enough," Noah smiled.

Renee came back with a whole tray. There was a gallon plastic jug of orange juice, which Corey upended into his mouth without any ceremony. She had also brought out a glass full of ice cubes and the bottle of green Gatorade for Noah, iced tea with mint for herself, and a plate of homemade peanut butter cookies. After Corey had gulped half the jug, he took a cookie. It was warm. "Did you make these?" he asked.

Renee loved to cook. "Yes."

Corey realized why she looked different. She wasn't wearing her glasses.

"They're fantastic," said Noah, stuffing a whole one into his mouth.

"Thank you!" she chirped. "That's my favorite recipe."

"I can see why," Noah said around a mouthful of crumbs. His conversation was a lot more charming than his table manners.

Feeling human again, Corey took a cookie. "Who called?" he asked.

Renee tasted one of her cookies. "These *are* good! It was Luke."

"What did he want? Why didn't you call me?"

"He didn't ask to talk to you. He asked if you were around and I said you were with Noah...."

"Uh-oh," Noah said.

"Stop it," said Corey. "What did he want?"

"I don't know. He said, 'Noah's over shooting hoops with Corey?' and I said, 'yes,' and I asked if he wanted to talk to you and he said he'd call sometime when you weren't busy."

"See?" Noah said. "You're in trouble now for consorting with the enemy."

"You don't know what you're talking about!"

"Corey!" said Renee. "You're screaming!"

"No, I'm not!" Corey screamed.

"I've done it again!" Noah said. "Everywhere I go it's World War III."

"Don't flatter yourself," Corey snarled.

"Are you online?" Renee asked Noah, turning her chair to exclude Corey.

"Yeah. AOL."

"What are your favorite Web sites?"

"The NBA has a great one. There's a sports chat room I like...."

"I like Amazon.com. And there's a chat room for *Athena*, which is my favorite show."

"*Athena*?" Noah said.

"The warrior Goddess," Renee clarified. "Haven't you seen it? It's the best."

Noah laughed. "It sounds strange."

"No, not really. She was Zeus's daughter. She sprang from his head...."

"Renee..." Corey said.

"No, I'm interested," Noah said. "What else do you like?" he asked Renee.

"Do you know there's a goth Web site?"

"Really? What's it got?"

She stood up, eyes sparkling. "I'll show you!"

"Renee!" Corey said. "Noah came over to play with me!" He was only half-kidding.

"I'll bring him back!" she said, taking Noah's hand.

Noah was laughing. "See you?" he said, shrugging at Corey as he was dragged off.

"What just happened?" Corey said to the empty yard.

A few minutes later, Beth came outside in her bathing suit with a bottle of suntan oil.

"You know what Renee's doing?" Corey said. "She's entertaining a man in her bedroom."

"Good for her!" Beth said. "Anybody I know?"

"It's a friend of mine, but you wouldn't know him since you don't come to my games."

She was slathering her arm, concentrating like a lover. "I had cramps."

"You have cramps every Friday night, Beth. I think Don should know about that before you guys try to have children."

"Look, Corey. I'm old enough now that I've earned the right to not go to stupid little family things."

"Hey, you need to say one more sentence. There's a little piece of my heart you didn't crush."

"Corey, I'm glad you're a big basketball star. Just don't bore me with it, okay?"

"Okay, if I don't have to go to your stupid wedding."

"I don't want you there, but I think Mom would be disappointed."

Corey sighed. He was too exhausted for this low-level sparring. He had bigger issues in his life. "Beth? Did you ever feel like you'd gotten into a situation where it didn't matter what you did, you just knew something awful was going to go down?"

"Yes. The day they brought you home from the hospital."

"Please. I'm serious. Obviously you can see I have no one to turn to or I wouldn't be asking you."

"Okay, what's your problem? Choosing between Clearasil and Stridex?" She grinned wickedly.

Corey took a slug of juice. "Forget it."

"No," she said. "I'm sorry. What's on your mind?"

"Well...how do you know what to believe? I mean how do you decide what's true?"

"Oh, Christ, is this about Catholicism? Ask Father Handrahan! I'm so pissed at the Church now I could—"

"Not about Catholicism. About people. Like if you decide to trust somebody, how do you know if you're wrong?"

"Who is this about?"

"Never mind. Just answer me."

She started working lotion into her legs. "The answer to that is really easy, Corey. When they betray you, you know you were wrong. If they never do, you know you were right."

Corey was stunned. "You mean that? You spend your whole life basically waiting to be betrayed?"

She looked at Corey over her sunglasses. "So far, that's the only system that's worked for me."

"Don't you trust Don?"

She laughed. "So far..."

"God!" Corey sat up. "I couldn't live like that! I have to believe that most people are good and you can pretty much take them at their word!"

Beth reclined and pulled her visor down over her eyes, signaling the conversation was over. "I know," she said. "I'm going to miss that about you, Corey. You always were the easiest person to screw over."

Chapter

Monday was strange in so many ways, Corey didn't know what to worry about first. Franny wouldn't make eye contact in homeroom. He ran after her in the hall and she told him she had to get home early tonight and wouldn't be at basketball practice. In first-period math, Luke was openly hostile, apparently because Corey had socialized with Noah

over the weekend. By the time they got to second-period religion, Corey was angry back at him. Were they married? Didn't Luke trust him? The reason he'd invited Noah over in the first place was to protect Luke. They glared at each other through the whole lecture on martyrs.

But lunch was the worst. Corey couldn't find anyone to eat with. The cafeteria was a ghost town: no Franny, no Luke, no Antawn, no Theo, no Noah. Ricky was eating with some guys Corey didn't know, so he just waved and sat at a table alone, self-consciously eating his chef's salad.

Fifth period he had American History and finally saw someone—Noah. "Where was everybody at lunch?" Corey exploded, because by that time he was working on a conspiracy theory.

Noah jumped back a little. "I was at McDonald's. I hate that cafeteria food."

That figured. "Did you go with anyone?"

Noah flushed. He had a funny expression, his pupils narrowing, as if Corey's question was a bright light. "Yeah. I was with a girl I'm interested in. Is that okay with you?"

Corey realized how he sounded. "I'm sorry. I couldn't find half the team at lunchtime. It creeped me out."

"Afraid of a mutiny, Captain?" Noah laughed.

For the first time, Corey could see why some people didn't like this guy. "No," he said in a controlled voice. "My first thought was that the whole team had taken you out somewhere and beaten you up."

Noah laughed, but his face was frowning. He was about to say something when Mr. Pruitt came in. Picking up his pen, Corey saw his hand was shaking a little. He hated confrontations.

Sixth period, both Antawn and Theo were missing from English. Now Corey was starting to panic. What if they were cutting school today? Today's practice was crucial. They had to get past Luke's accident and pull the team together again. Friday's game was Dillard, a squad so big and bad they would make St. Anthony seem like a croquet match. It was early in the season to have such a crucial game and even if things were good, it would be dicey. And things weren't that good.

Mr. Hubbard droned on about *Madame Bovary* and Corey's mind ran rampant with fantasies. What if Noah had drugged Luke and was systematically drugging other members of the team? Maybe he took them all out to McDonald's and slipped them something in their Cokes. Corey would be, like, an accessory because he'd suspected something but hadn't told anybody. If he found out either Antawn or Theo had gotten sick today, he'd tell. He'd tell everything.

"Mr. Brennan?" Mr. Hubbard was smiling maliciously.

This was the favorite trick of every teacher since Plato. Find a student who's daydreaming and ask them a question. They just never tired of it.

Corey sighed. "Could you repeat the question?"

Mr. Hubbard made some loving adjustments in his ratty cardigan sweater, which he always wore, even when it was a hundred degrees outside. Antawn believed he was hiding something in there—possibly breasts. "What do you feel Emma Bovary was really in search of?"

"Guys," Corey said, proving he was way off his game.

Mr. Hubbard pursed his lips.

"I mean…what they represented."

Mr. Hubbard smiled, baring his wolfish teeth. He liked Corey. All English teachers liked Corey because he understood and was willing to talk their talk. "And what do you think men represented to her?"

Corey struggled to remember the book through his mass of other worries. "I think she was one of those people who are never happy with what they have. So she always thought a new guy would change her life, but then it would get old and she'd have to do something else."

"Excellent, Mr. Brennan. Excellent! Can anyone think of a parallel to our modern society?"

Luckily, Blanca Garcia could, so the spotlight shifted off Corey.

Finally the bell rang, and Corey almost ran out of the room. He was jogging toward the gym, when something snagged his sleeve and almost took him off his feet. It was Antawn. He pulled Corey into an empty classroom and closed the door. "Talk to him, man!" he raved. "He's crazy!"

Antawn was pointing at Theo, who sat slumped on a teacher's stool that was much too small for him. His massive shoulders were pulled in protectively, like birds' wings. His head was down.

At first Corey thought Theo was ashamed about something, but when his voice came out it was low and tight with anger. "We can talk about this at practice."

"No!" Antawn circled him, pointing a finger in his face. "That's too easy! You look Corey in the eye and tell him what you want to do!"

"What's going on here?" Corey said. "We're going to be late. Where have you guys been all day?"

Antawn turned to Corey. "We been arguing all day about what this crazy man want to do to destroy all of us!" He pivoted toward Theo again. "Because he just like his name. A stone. He got no feelings. He don't care...."

Theo's head came up slowly, like a bull getting ready to charge. "Hey!" he thundered.

"Okay, okay!" Corey said quickly. "Theo, tell me what's going on."

Antawn pitched himself into a chair and folded his arms. "Well? Tell him."

Theo started a couple of times and cleared his throat. "I'm sorry, Corey," he whispered.

Corey turned to Antawn in horror. Was Theo Stone, six feet three and 235 pounds, getting ready to cry? Antawn had softened now and seemed to realize his buddy couldn't get the words out. "He wants to quit the team."

Corey's head felt hollow, like when he hadn't eaten enough. "Huh?"

"I'm sorry," Theo said again. He was squeezing his hands together in his lap.

Antawn got up again. "You can't do this to us, Stonehenge. You can't. We need you. You're the best guard we'll ever have. This is our senior year. You want to blow your scholarship and our championship?" He was windmilling his arm in Corey's direction, apparently urging him to jump into this.

"Tell me what's wrong," Corey said. "Whatever it is, we can fix it. You want a bigger gym? Your own hot tub in the locker room? Women? Tell me. I swear I'll get it for you."

Theo laughed a little and looked up. His eyes looked ancient and sad. "It's nothing like that. I don't want anything. I just think this is the best thing for me to do."

Antawn's arms went limp at his sides. "That's all you gonna get, Corey. I've been ragging on him all day and I'm supposed to be his best friend and that's all I can get. What kind of thing can't you tell your best friend?"

"Let it go," Theo said to him. "Please."

"Is this about Noah?" Corey said.

Theo looked up too quickly. "Noah? Why would it be about Noah?"

"Well…Noah has some kind of idea the black guys on the team think he's a racist."

"Only cause he is!" Antawn said. "And if that mother ever says one wrong word to me—"

"Whether or not he's a racist is Antawn's problem, not mine," Theo interrupted. "I don't think about him one way or the other. If he was David Duke he wouldn't keep me off my own team. I'd just deal with it. Listen, Corey. Listen."

He lowered his voice. "This is something about me. Just about me. And it's personal. And I hate it and you're making me feel awful with all this. Can't we just go to practice and let me tell the squad, and then I can go home and feel bad by myself? Antawn's been on my case all day with this. I can't take much more."

There was something in Theo's dark eyes that was so vulnerable it made Corey look away. "We're just torturing him, Antawn," he said quietly. "He's already made up his mind."

The locker room scene was even worse. It was like Theo had told them he only had a few months to live. Luke even forgot to be mad at Corey in the wake of this bigger crisis. "We need you to protect our scores!" he pleaded, actually holding his arms out to Theo.

Theo had gone deaf, blind, and mute right after he made his announcement. He sat by his locker with his head lowered while they all took shots at him.

Landis was obviously close to tears. "It would help if you tell us why. I've been coaching ten years and I never heard of a player who wants to quit the team. I know you, man. You love basketball. If you're having a problem with someone on the squad..."

"No problem on the squad," Theo said.

"Is there a problem at home? Something you want to talk to me about privately? Because we can work out—"

"No problem at home. No problem with the squad. No problem with the weather. No problem with the world situation. Just don't want to play anymore."

This was part of what made him such a valuable guard.

He knew how to put up a wall. "Is there anything we can say..." Corey began.

"What else can you say?" Theo got up so suddenly, several people jumped back from him. "People have been talking at me all day. I'm done talking." He headed for the door. "I'll come back later to get my things and give you my key, Mr. Landis."

"Okay," Landis said to a slamming door.

They all looked at each other. "We have to respect his decision," Landis said. "Antawn, try to be there for him. If he wants to talk about it and you find out it's something we can make right..."

Antawn was shaking his head vigorously. "This is something big and bad. That boy would never quit this team unless it was something awful. It's got to be his family or maybe he's sick...maybe a doctor told him..."

"Look, we shouldn't speculate behind his back," Landis said. "We're just gossiping at this point. He's eighteen years old and we can't make him play and we can't make him talk about it. All we can do is be available and let him know he has a place here if he wants to come back."

"Right," Corey said. "And we have to fill the gaping 235 pound hole he just made in our defense."

"It's like we're cursed!" Antawn said, glancing at Noah. "First Luke, and now this!"

"Well, I'm fine," Luke said. "And Corey's right. We've got Dillard on Friday and we've gotta make up this deficit."

"We've got to move Noah up," Corey said. "We need all the power we can get in our starting lineup."

"That's right," Landis said to Noah. "You're too valuable

to sit on the bench at this point."

"Isn't it the weirdest thing!" Antawn said. "Every time we have bad luck, Noah comes out good!"

Corey laid a very gentle hand on Antawn's arm. "You're upset right now, be careful what you say."

Antawn shook himself, as if to throw off his mood. "It's true, though," he muttered.

Noah ignored Antawn. "I'll play any position where I can help the team," he said.

"Great," Landis said. "Now how do we want to reshuffle? Corey? Ideas?"

Corey could see in his peripheral vision that Luke and Noah were staring at him from opposite sides, very much like the two velociraptors in *Jurassic Park* who ate the big-game hunter.

"We could go two ways, I guess," he said. "The obvious thing is to put Antawn back on guard because he's played it before and put Noah in as the other forward, but if you want my opinion, it would be better to leave Antawn on offense and let Noah be the guard."

Luke's hostile gaze was withdrawn. Noah's intensified. "How do you figure that, Corey?" Noah said in a shaky voice. "That gives you two men who aren't playing their natural position. I'm really a center, you know."

"That job's taken!" Luke shouted.

Corey held out a hand to Luke to stop him. He turned to Noah. "You said you'd play any position to help the team."

"Well, yeah, sure, but—"

Corey spoke to Landis now. "I played one-on-one with Noah over the weekend. He's a fantastic guard. And he's big. If we have two relatively small guys on defense, those big forwards at Dillard will plow them down. Plus, look at what a great offensive job Antawn did in the game against St. Tony's. I mean, who cares what anybody played in the past? We need to put everybody in where they can do the most good now."

"I think you're absolutely right," Landis said. "That's an excellent strategy, Corey. I'm proud of you. Everybody good with that?"

"Works for me," Luke said, giving Corey an all-is-forgiven smile.

"Noah, you know how important defense is," Landis continued. "And there's nothing that throws the opponents off more than a guard who can shoot."

Everyone looked at Noah. He was holding Corey's eyes with an expression Corey couldn't read. "Like I said, whatever's good for the team."

***

They had a great practice. Corey had been right about the lineup; they all meshed beautifully, except for a little problem getting Luke and Noah to pass to each other, but that was a minor point. By the time he got home, Corey was starting to feel Theo hadn't killed the all-city for them after all.

After dinner, Beth went out, and Corey didn't feel like watching TV with his parents, so he decided to try to crash Renee's private domain. She spent every evening in her room talking to her E-mail pals. Corey listened at her door for a few seconds. The soft tap of keys sounded like water flowing over seashells. He knocked.

"Just a minute." There was some rather rapid tapping and the hum of a save or an exit. Then, "Come in."

Corey came in and sat on the edge of the bed, trying to ignore the gargoyles and ghouls that stared down from her posters. "You should learn to ask who it is," he chided. "Beth could get in."

"Beth doesn't knock." Renee switched off her screen and put her glasses on top of her head. "You're actually the only one in the family with any manners."

"Proving Beth's theory that I'm adopted. So what did you cover up just before I came in? Are you already at the age of downloading porn?"

She laughed. "Shut up! Are you kidding? That stuff is disgusting and it's all set up for men."

Corey leaned on his elbow. "You're cleverly not answering my question."

She laughed again, not quite her natural one. "I was in a chat room."

"What's his name?"

"Shut up!"

"Come on, Renee. Don't hold out. Just cause you're blossoming into womanhood..."

"I shouldn't have let you in!"

"...doesn't mean you can't share everything with your brother."

"All right, but don't get a bunch of ideas like that I'm meeting perverts in the park, okay?"

"I know the difference between you and Beth."

"Okay." She shifted in her chair. "Okay. There's a kid I've

been talking to. A guy. He likes all the same things I like."

"Well, I'm sure it's really an old guy in a raincoat, but as long as you keep it verbal, what's his name?"

Her mouth twisted into a silly smile that looked completely alien. "Gareth."

"Gareth!"

"That's his *goth* name."

"Oh! His *goth* name."

"If you're going to make fun of me... You know, I don't tease you about the fact that all you date are brainless bimbos."

"Good point. Don't tease me about that. Anyway, the current brainless bimbo is avoiding me. But let's keep the focus on Gareth. Now, are you a goth, too? Or are you a Lombard or a Saxon or something?"

"It's a gothic chat room. I've told you about it. It's called Dungeon 6."

"Such a sweet little girl you are!"

"We talk about the Arthurian Legend. He recommended this outrageous book on Queen Mab."

"Who?"

"You don't know your own roots, Corey. This is the stuff they don't tell you in school."

"Probably so we'll lay off the human sacrifices. So, tell me, Queen Mab, do you have a gothic name you use in this chat room?"

"Ygraine."

"Come again?"

"Ygraine. She was King Arthur's mother."

"Oh, yes. That Ygraine. You know this whole conversation

is kind of giving me an Ygraine."

"I wouldn't really expect a jock to understand any of this."

"Hey! I'm a pretty intellectual jock. I just read *Madame Bovary*!"

"Yeah, right. With all the dirty parts underlined."

"Well, I'm still your big brother, even if I am a dumb, horny jock. You know you want to keep this thing just on the screen, right?"

"What are you talking about?"

"You know what I'm talking about. Does Gareth live here, locally?"

"I don't even know! Probably not. Did you see some kind of story on Channel Seven?"

"I care about you, Lady Ygraine. Even if you are highly intellectual and possess supernatural powers, you're just thirteen and there's a lot of bad boys out there. I know, because I'm one of them."

"I can take care of myself, Corey."

"Okay." He paused. "Guess what? Theo Stone quit the team."

"Are you kidding? Why?"

"That's the bothersome part. The Stone is stonewalling. It's either that he hates Noah—"

"I like Noah!"

"I know you do. But Antawn and Luke don't like him and they have good radar, too. But I don't think Theo would quit over personalities. He gets along with everybody. He wouldn't give us a reason, like there was a deep dark secret he couldn't tell."

"Maybe he has a heart condition."

"That theory came up. But we have exams all the time. Can you just get a bad heart out of the blue?"

"I don't know. What are you going to do?"

"Move Noah up to first string guard."

"Good."

"Can you be on the team, Renee? You always like my decisions."

She laughed. "Is Luke still mad?"

"No, I made Noah mad by making him a guard, and that made Luke happy. It's kind of like the tilting planes of geometry."

"What would a jock know about that?" She smiled, and in some kind of ghostly way, she suddenly looked much older.

"Well, I'll let you get back to the middle ages." Corey stood up. He felt better. Ten minutes with Renee was better than an hour in the whirlpool.

"Corey?"

He paused at the door.

The woman-smile flashed again. "That was sweet, the way you were trying to look out for me."

He closed the door and leaned against it for several seconds, listening to the computer hum and sing as it booted up again. Then came the soft, rhythmic tapping. Corey wished his world could be like that.

Chapter

Dillard was an away game, which carried a special energy all its own. There was a pep rally in the gym beforehand, whose real purpose was to pump up some St. Philip's kids so they would get on the buses and make a cheering section in the hostile Dillard crowd.

Coach Landis was the emcee of these events, which  brought out some kind of weird extroversion he never had in normal life. He always insisted on the teams being there and they had to be introduced one by one and get a little individualized cheer from the cheerleaders: first the freshmen team, then the girls' varsity, then the boys. As usual, Corey felt he was shortchanged. All the guys had great cheers except him. For Luke they did "Doctor, Doctor Send Us the Cure." For Antawn it was called "Bad Boy." For Theo, "Like a Rock." They kept changing Corey's cheer, as if they knew they weren't getting it right. Last year, it was some crap about having "heart." Now it was a monotonous chant about "simply the best." It was just like the nickname. Corey wondered if he was lacking something the other guys had—like a personality.

The cheerleaders were looking exceptionally buff. They considered the Dillard Squad to be stiff competition and always gave it a little extra. Letitia, for instance, had beaded her hair. As she bounced and swayed, the beads clicked like castanets.

Franny, for her part, had a shiny French braid and was

wearing non-regulation panties in a bright Badger red. The first time she jumped in the air, Corey saw them and smiled to himself. He had to force himself to stop thinking about it.

Tonight was weird because they had no Theo. As they drilled, Corey thought he missed the sound of those size-sixteen shoes scudding around him. He'd kind of hoped Theo would at least come to the game and sit on the bench or in the audience, but he wasn't at the rally. Also missing was Corey's family. Beth never came, but his parents usually did. They were meeting instead with Beth's caterer, which she insisted had to be done on a Friday night. The wedding was going to be a disaster, Corey could see. She wanted a harvest theme which sounded to Corey like she was going to mow Don down with a machete. She was having gourds and squashes everywhere and the wedding cake was supposed to be pumpkin-flavored—ugh! Corey thought the orchestra should play, "Don't Fear the Reaper."

The real disappointment tonight was Renee. She had never missed a game of Corey's in four years, but tonight she wanted to stay home in hopes of talking to her white knight in the chat room. Corey was really hurt, but he gave himself a lecture about it. She was thirteen. She couldn't tag around after Corey forever, worshipping him, pleasant as that was.

It was close to game time now. Landis was winding the rally down, starting to give lectures on how to behave on the buses and that they were all representatives of the school, etc., etc. Luke was absentmindedly holding the ball, and Noah expertly swatted it out of his hands, zigzagged to the basket, and double-pumped it in.

"I hate him," Luke muttered to Corey.

"You hate Dillard," Corey corrected. "Noah's on our side."

"That remains to be seen," Luke said. He spotted Claire across the gym practicing free throws, and sprinted off. Corey watched them kiss for several seconds and decided he wanted to talk to Franny.

He came up behind her and covered her eyes, guess-who style. She didn't guess, just worked her way loose and spun around. Corey saw something in her eyes. It looked like she'd been hoping Corey was someone else. "Oh, hi," she said.

"Hi!" Corey tried not to show he was mad. "Sorry to bother you."

She exchanged some significant glances with her friends. "Let's go out in the hall for a minute," she said. "I want to talk to you." She took him by the wrist and led him. A chorus of catcalls followed them.

Corey could tell this wasn't going to be a friendly meeting. Well, good. He knew she was mad about something. Get it in the open, he could fake an apology and get on with life.

"Sit down," she said. "I don't like getting a stiff neck talking to you."

That pissed him off, but he held it in and sat on the edge of a bench while she stood over him with her arms folded. "You're a very nice guy, Corey..." she began.

Oh, no! "Franny, wait. I've got a game. Whatever it is—"

"I think it's time to start seeing other people."

Something like a landslide started happening in Corey's chest. He was surprised at his own reaction to this. For the last couple of months he'd had to admit to himself he didn't really like Franny all that well, but he stayed with her because she was so sexy. But right now he felt like that Christmas when they gave him a puppy and he had to give it back the next day because Beth was allergic. "Tell me what I did," he heard himself say. "Maybe we can fix it."

She looked very blurry all of a sudden. This was bad. Crying before a game would be very, very bad.

"I don't want to fix it, Corey. I feel tied down. I want to have fun while I'm young, date other boys…"

"What magazine did you get this crap from!" Corey stood up so fast, Franny jumped back and touched her heart. "How dare you do this to me right before the Dillard game! What's his name?" Being this angry was a relief. You can't cry when you're yelling and screaming.

Franny took another step back and crossed her arms again, like a shield. "You're being abusive, Corey, and the discussion is over. Please be mature…."

For some reason the red panties crossed Corey's mind just at that second, like a final stab to the heart. "Who did you put that underwear on for, you—"

"Okay!" she held up her hands. "I was hoping you'd be an adult about it. I was wrong."

Kids were coming out of the gym now, heading for the buses. They streamed around Corey and Franny, a few glancing over with interest. To Corey's horror, the tears were back, burning his eyes. He swung around to face the wall, feeling like an animal in a trap.

"Hey!" Luke's arm looped around his neck, his body shielding Corey from onlookers. "What's up?"

Corey shook his head violently. Any retelling of the story would break him down. Luke pulled open the men's room door, steering Corey with the other hand. Some little nerd with glasses was in there washing up. "Get lost!" Luke thundered. The kid ran out like he was scalded.

"I'm okay." Corey tried to duck past Luke and get back out the door, but Luke knew how to block.

"What is it, Cor?"

"We've gotta go! We have to get on the bus!"

"The bus isn't going anyplace without us," Luke pointed out. "What happened? What did she say to you?"

Corey stared at a urinal. "She broke up with me," he said.

"Right now? Before a game?"

Corey sighed. "Thank you. If this is her idea of being a good cheerleader..." He tried to laugh but it sounded like a little kid with asthma trying to breathe.

Luke, meanwhile, was eyeing him like a paramedic. Corey could read his mind. *What's the damage? Can he play?* "You know what I've always thought of her."

"Yeah. You were right. I mean, I don't even know how much I liked her, but I kind of loved her. You know?"

"No. That's nuts."

"She's got another guy," Corey felt the anger rising again. "Did you see her underwear? She's wearing some kind of 'come get me' underwear for SOME OTHER GUY!" He punctuated the last three words by banging on the hand dryer.

Luke grabbed the hand and held it suspended. "What do you care? You could get anybody. You could do so much better, Corey."

There was a knock on the door. "Luke? Corey?" Landis called. "Are you in there?"

"Yeah, just a second," Luke called.

"You're not getting sick again, are you?" Landis's voice went soprano.

That made them both laugh. "No!" Luke called. "We'll be there in a minute."

Luke let go of Corey's hand. They looked at each other. "I'm okay," Corey said. "Really. This won't affect my game."

Luke pulled Corey against him and immediately pushed him away, more like a collision than a hug. "It's okay," he grinned. "I'll cover for you if you suck."

"Like hell you will!" Corey checked his face in the mirror and they went out.

Together.

There were two buses, one for the proletariat and one for the players and cheerleaders. Franny was up front, surrounded by her loyal squad, who all seemed to have heard her version of the story, because they glared at Corey. Luke loyally stepped on her foot as they went past. "Whoops! Sorry, honey!" he said.

"Ouch!" she cried. "You clumsy ox!"

The girls' team always sat in the middle of the bus, the boys' in the back. Claire glanced up when Luke and Corey came down the aisle. She obviously saw something in their faces that made her jump up and follow. They went to the last seat in the bus, Luke on one side of Corey, Claire on the other. Corey thought they were acting like packing material, transporting something fragile. "That witch!" Claire whispered to Corey. "How could she do that to you before a game?"

Apparently everybody knew about this. Kids were sneaking glances back at Corey.

"She's got somebody else; I know it," he said in a low voice.

"Get off of that," Luke lectured him. "Why should you care if she does?"

"You were always too good for her," Claire agreed. She was pressing up against him, just like Luke was on the other side and Corey understood it was just some kind of bolstering gesture, but she didn't feel the same as Luke. Not at all.

***

Everything about Dillard was intimidating. The school itself was old, big, and cavernous. Pictures of their mascot, a springing black panther, were everywhere. It was hard for Antawn to even trash talk them. After all, what's a badger next to a bunch of panthers? He was usually reduced to weak taunts like, "Here come the dullards from Dillard." Their reserve bench had been awesome last year, one of the few teams to defeat St. Philip's. Now they were seniors and looked even scarier. They were huge, for one thing, and they had a kind of silent, proud way about them that was worse than rowdiness. Most of them came from poorer families than the St. Philip's kids. They had something to prove.

The early games went for St. Philip though. The freshmen beat Dillard 50–35, and Claire's team beat the Dillard girls 62–60. Corey knew that would make their game all the harder. The Panther varsity boys were mad.

Corey's personal nightmare was the point guard, James Wright III. He was about six foot five to Corey's six foot two, about 260 to Corey's 170 and he lifted weights for a hobby. He growled when he played—not a grunt, but a real growl, and he loved to throw the elbow. Corey had bruises on his face last year after the Dillard game. Right now, James Wright III was staring at Corey from the Dillard bench. Just like a real panther—a hungry one—might stare at a real badger. Already shaken, Corey couldn't seem to look away.

Apparently, Antawn saw this and came to the rescue. "What the *hell* you looking at, boy?" he shouted.

JWIII calmly shifted his gaze to Antawn. "Who you calling boy, boy?"

Antawn pointed at him. "I'm calling you boy, boy! Quit turning this way. Your ugly face is scaring my team."

James Wright III smiled and slumped lower on the bench, like a crocodile sliding into water. "Why don't you come over this way, you skinny—"

"Your mother is so ugly when she walks past the men's room all the zippers go back up!" Antawn shrieked.

"Okay!" Landis put his body between the two benches. "That's enough." He encouraged some of this, but always reined Antawn in if he thought it was going too far.

Corey turned his attention away and struggled to focus. This was going to be a hard game and he had to stay in the moment. He tried to listen to the flow of sound around him, but his mind was jumpy, wondering who Franny was seeing, thinking about James Wright III and his big, heavy elbows....

It was already game time! Luke was praying, Landis was moving along behind the bench giving each player his last word. He whispered "Cooperate," to Luke. To Corey he whispered "Concentrate." Corey jumped. Did his lack of concentration show that much? That made it seem hopeless. The buzzer sounded. Corey almost screamed. He did multiplication tables in his head as the players were called onto the court and they had to say his name twice.

Dillard got the tip and Corey gamely tried to contain JWIII while Noah somehow executed a turnaround and passed to Corey. *Concentrate!* Corey pivoted, ducked under the swinging boom of Wright's arm and headed for the goal. Antawn was somehow there, and open. St. Philip was on the board.

Dillard came right back and got their first field goal. Noah picked it up and dribbled to St. Philip's goal, where Luke was wide open, but Noah passed to Corey, who couldn't even see the ball around Wright's octopus arms. Wright got it, passed it to one of their hotshot forwards and off they went.

"What's your problem?" Corey heard Luke yell at Noah as they ran downcourt. Noah acted like he hadn't heard. This time, after Dillard scored, taking the lead, Luke almost pushed Noah out of the way, took the ball himself all the way upcourt, and slammed it in.

"Don't play against each other!" Corey warned them. He wondered if they should call a time-out. On their next play, just to get on the board, Corey let JWIII smash an elbow into his face, and took the two easy free throws. Landis called a time-out, took Corey out and put Tim White in.

"What are you doing?" Corey cried in horror. "I'm fine and Luke and Noah aren't passing to each other!"

"That's the point," Landis said, watching grimly. "If you're out of the game for a minute, maybe those two clowns will work together."

Five minutes later, with St. Philip down by six points, Landis conceded his plan didn't work and put Corey back in. Dillard had already picked up on the fact that Corey was the only player everyone seemed to pass to and began to double-team him, as if that was necessary with Mr. Wright on the case. In desperation, Corey started throwing himself into his guards like a whale trying to beach itself. He actually tied the game with free throws, getting dizzy from the hits he was taking, while Noah and Luke glared at each other like a couple of real badgers. At the halftime buzzer, Noah threw a Hail Mary and got three points, letting them go into the break in the lead, but to Corey's mind, this didn't make up for the fact that he probably had permanent brain damage. The sight of Franny bouncing out onto the floor in her red panties only added fuel to his fire. As they gathered on the bench, Corey started Landis's speech for him. "Look, you two idiots," he shouted, "I don't care if you murder each other off the court, but this is Dillard, and we're going to blow it if you don't start acting like a team. It's not like I'm not flattered that you all want to pass to me but you're getting me killed!" He picked up a piece of ice and held it to his face for emphasis. "Now look, we can come out of the half and use this. They think I'm the only shooter and they've got the whole pack on me. That means both of you two will probably be really open in the first few minutes. Please, please, pass to each other so we can win this game. Please." Corey didn't even wait for an answer. He stalked off, deciding he didn't want to hear anything they had to say, and he definitely didn't want to watch the halftime entertainment.

"Corey, I'm sorry!" Luke called after him.

"You ought to be," Landis said, and started his own harangue.

Corey walked out into the hallways of Dillard, past the kids using phones and Coke machines, past the posters of leaping panthers, until he found a shadowy hall to call his own. He fantasized about a hot whirlpool. It felt like one of those guards had kicked him in the small of his back. He leaned over, trying to stretch the muscle.

"Corey?"

He turned and saw a lithe, graceful silhouette coming toward him. It was Claire in her uniform, pulling the rubber band out of her hair. She sprinted to him, her blond hair flying like ribbons, and stopped in front of him, panting a little. Her cheeks were flushed and her blue eyes were bright. Corey felt the urge to cry coming back and this time he wasn't even sure why.

"Are you okay?" she said.

He ran his hand over his hair, trying to shore up the contents of his head. "Yeah, yeah. Those guards were beating the crap out of me. I just wanted to..." Something about her big sympathetic eyes was destroying him. "I didn't want to watch Franny...." he said softly as he let his sore body sag against the wall.

"Oh, Corey." She came and put her arms around him. She smelled lemony. "Don't let her do this to you."

Lemons and baby powder and maybe something else— like clean kitten fur. Corey knew he should push her away, but he didn't. She was so comforting and he really needed to be comforted. "It's not just her," he said, letting his cheek rest against her hair. "I'm tired. My team won't play together and those guys are beating me up and my whole house is in an uproar with the wedding...." A warm tear slid down his face and caught in Claire's hair like a raindrop in a spiderweb. He let himself squeeze her harder.

She should have objected, but for some reason she didn't. "You'll find somebody better," she was saying. She bent her head and rubbed her cheek against his chest. "Every girl in the school wants you."

Corey suddenly remembered Noah telling him he thought Claire liked him. He'd never considered the possibility since she and Luke seemed so married. He drew a sharp breath, thinking how dangerous this was if they both liked each other. The last thing he needed...

"If I wasn't involved with Luke..." she began and suddenly looked up, clearly offering her mouth for a kiss. Her mouth was small, soft, unlipsticked.

"Shhhh." Corey pulled her against him, forcing her to lower her head again. "Luke is so lucky," he whispered into her hair. He wanted one last deep breath of lemon-powder-kitten and then he planned to push her away.

But then he felt it. Without looking up. It was like his mother said, the feeling you get when someone walks over your grave. He slowly released Claire and looked down into the shadows, where he saw a silhouette he knew as well as his own.

"You scum," Luke said quietly.

Chapter

Luke sprang. Corey didn't even move to defend himself. He just felt the slam as they hit the floor together. *More injuries.* He looked up at his best friend's red face. Luke's blond forelock dripped sweat into Corey's eyes. The St. Luke medal swung crazily. Then Corey noticed he couldn't breathe because instead of punching him, Luke had locked

his fingers on Corey's throat. *This is serious.* Corey was horrified at his own defective calm.

Meanwhile, Claire was beating her fists uselessly on Luke's back. Corey knew he had to try a groin kick or something. He worked an arm free and grabbed the St. Luke's medal, pulling it toward his mouth like he was going to bite it. Sure enough, Luke's piety was stronger than his rage. He broke his hold and wrenched the medal out of Corey's hand, jumping off him. Corey was glad he knew his opponent so well. Luke might not have stopped for pain, but he wouldn't let anybody desecrate his saint.

Corey stayed on the ground. His throat felt like bricks were piled on it and something was wrong with his back. He tried to speak, to explain he was innocent, but it all came out as hideous gagging sounds.

Luke, meanwhile, had whirled on Claire with his unspent rage. "What were you doing? What the hell do you think you were doing?"

She was wisely backing away and bumped into Landis, who had obviously come looking for his lost sheep. Corey wondered what time it was. It would be horrible to forfeit.

Landis surveyed the scene with wide eyes. "What in the world is going on here?"

Claire fled.

Before they could even answer, Landis had put his hands on Luke's shoulders, as if sensing he needed comfort and restraint.

Corey struggled and sat up. He coughed like an elderly wino. "I'm okay," he rasped. "I can still play."

"You bastard!" Luke said to Corey, looking ready to lunge again. "You bastard! How could you?..." Tears suddenly appeared in Luke's eyes. This was more about the friendship than Claire, Corey realized.

"You're wrong," Corey wheezed, trying to stand. His back was killing him. He looked at Landis and tried to stand straight. "He saw me with Claire and he thought... I was upset and she put her arms around me. That's all. But he..." Corey felt himself blushing. It wasn't the whole truth. He and Claire had both betrayed Luke in their thoughts.

"Liar!" Luke's voice was ragged and childish. "He's a liar!"

"Hey! What's going on in here?" It was Coach Martin from the Panthers. Now they were really busted.

"We had a little misunderstanding," Landis said, letting go of Luke. "But it's over now. They're going to shake hands and go back out and play. Right, guys?"

"Right." Corey walked toward Luke, feeling burned by those staring blue eyes. He held out a visibly shaking hand.

For several agonizing seconds, it looked like Luke was going to refuse. Then he glanced at the coaches, listlessly pressed and released Corey's hand, and immediately turned and walked back toward the gym.

Mr. Martin was smiling. "Good luck in the second half!" he said, slapping Landis on the shoulder.

"Back at you, you..." Landis muttered. He looked at Corey. "I think I should take you out. You look pretty beat up. Did he hit you?"

"No!" Corey said, which was the technical truth. "I'm fine. I'm good to go."

Landis put his arm around Corey's shoulder. "Where did we go wrong?" he asked as they walked out on the gym floor together. It was ironic that just as he said that, Noah, on the bench, caught Corey's eye and smiled.

***

Sun-Sentinel
NOAH'S ARC CAN'T SAVE
EMBATTLED BADGERS

The Dillard Panthers smashed a hole in the St. Philip juggernaut last night, coming back after a slow first half to shellac, wax, and spank the Badgers by a score of 72–43. Not to take anything away from a splendid offense, led by Jamal Jones and Ray Walker, I gotta say this one the Badgers lost through their own misguided efforts. Last year, this squad was legendary for a pick-and-roll as fine as the NBA, and a sense of teamwork that was the envy of other schools. What's up, guys? Last night, there was virtually no passing. I mean no passing. It looked like every man for himself and the formidable Dillard defense jumped on that weakness like a cat on a dish of milk.

Something's up with these Badgers. Nobody's talking, including the coach. Suddenly, Theo Stone is missing from the bench, Corey Brennan looked to be *limping* last night, and the whole team avoids eye contact with each other. Such a waste!

The only bright spot on the Badger horizon is newcomer Noah Travers who can shoot the 3-pointer like nobody else. But fancy tricks don't win games. A lot of people had high hopes for St. Philip to go all-city this season. I suggest, ladies and gentlemen, you go with your second choice. Maybe Dillard.

Corey wondered if this was what a hangover felt like. His head pounded, his stomach churned, his mind refused to focus. He mindlessly read the article over and over, wondering if the coaches at UM, where he had a full scholarship, were reading it and reconsidering.

Wondering how he could have lost his best friend and his girlfriend all in one night. Wondering how they could have played such a dismal game. Wondering how long the big black fingerprints on his neck were going to be visible. Wondering what could possibly happen next.

To answer his question, Beth came in the breakfast room and poured herself a cup of coffee. "How'd the game go?" she asked.

Corey laughed, a feeble madman's laugh.

"Oh!" She came to a full stop and peered at him. "You lost?"

"Yes," he said. "Yes, we did." He felt like crying. It might be fun to just crack up. No responsibility. Just a nice nurse, maybe with big boobs, spooning pudding into your mouth in a clean, white room.

"Please don't forget the rehearsal is Thursday night," she said, apparently having exhausted her tiny supply of empathy. "Have you picked which of your worthless friends you want to have at the wedding?"

Corey laughed again. "I don't have any friends," he said. "Oh, wait. I guess Antawn is still my friend. But the wedding is still a week away."

She sat down at the table with him, her brow furrowed with the effort of thinking about Corey's life instead of her own. "What are you trying to say?"

Corey enunciated slowly and clearly. "I have no friends."

"What about your slut girlfriend? What about that big moron, Luke?"

"Bethy, I'm really touched by your kind words, but...well, if you must know, the slut is seeing somebody else and the big moron tried to kill me last night."

Finally, Beth looked at the marks on his throat. "Oh, God!"

"And then we lost the game," Corey concluded.

She took her seldom-seen glasses out of the pocket of her robe and looked at Corey's neck again. "Luke really did that to you?"

Corey knew he'd hit bottom. For Beth to show him concern, well, it meant he was beyond pathetic. "He thought I was putting a move on his girlfriend."

"Were you?"

Corey lowered his eyes. "Not quite."

"Is that why you lost? Because you had a fight?"

"It didn't help anybody's game, that's for sure. See, Noah won't pass the ball to Luke. And now Luke won't pass to

Noah or to me. Antawn won't pass to Noah. And Theo's gone. We were about as coordinated as a bunch of sheep crossing the highway."

"I'm sorry, Corey. I really didn't follow that, but I'm really sorry. Why don't you talk this all over with Renee?" It was well-known in the family that Renee was Corey's personal therapist.

"She's busy. She wouldn't even go running with me this morning. Her Prince Charming logged on early this morning and they're tapping away together."

"Weird. At least it keeps her out of trouble."

"Yeah. The younger generation. When I was her age, I was sneaking around the drugstore looking for dirty magazines."

Beth laughed. "When I was her age, I thought I was going to become a nun. Oh!" She touched her headful of rollers. "I should have taken those out ten minutes ago. Now I'm going to be too curly!" She jumped up and rushed off.

Now there was a loss for the monastic world, Corey thought. He searched the house in vain for parents—why were they always gone these days? It was like they'd gotten tired of waiting for the kids to leave home and just took off themselves. He listened at Renee's door, but there was no break in the tapping. He called Antawn's house, but Antawn's mother said he went to see Theo, and Corey wasn't going to call over there. Corey roamed the house like a dog, wanting to howl with loneliness. Finally, he threw in the towel and called Noah. Who else did he have left?

***

Corey and Luke practically smacked into each other in the hall Monday morning going to homeroom. They both jumped back excessively, which reactivated Corey's back pain. Then they both came forward and almost collided again. "We have to talk," Corey said.

Luke shook his head. "Nothing to say."

"Luke, even if we're not friends anymore, we have to play together."

"Don't worry about it." Luke tried to shoulder past, but Corey blocked him. "Look," Luke said, "I was rattled Friday night, for good reason, but I can play with a team no matter how I feel about any individuals." He tried to surge forward again.

Corey blocked again. "Luke, I didn't do anything wrong. I swear to you. I wouldn't."

Luke took Corey's shoulders and moved him, gently, aside. "I don't want to hear it."

"Just meet me for lunch or before practice or something. Please?"

"After practice," Luke said over his shoulder. "When everybody's gone."

Corey sighed. It was going to be a long day. He and Luke sat through religion class—David and Jonathon—without Luke ever making eye contact. The lunchroom was just as deserted as last week. Corey had the horrible fear everyone was having secret meetings talking about him.

Antawn and Theo were silent and subdued all through English. Then, out in the hall, they watched Theo walk the wrong way: toward the parking lot, not the gym.

"We're all sitting under a bad star right now," Antawn

sighed. "It's like nothing can go right."

"It is like that," Corey agreed, still gazing after Theo. His gait looked sad somehow, like a big, old bear. "How is he?"

"Now he wants to drop out of St. Phil and go to Northwest," Antawn said.

Theo lived in the Northwest school district, and his family were Baptists, but his grandmother had enrolled him at St. Philip because she thought Theo could get a better education there. "What's he want to do that for?" Corey said, also thinking that he didn't want to find himself guarded by somebody like Theo when they played Northwest.

Antawn shrugged. "At least if he plays for them he can probably hang onto his scholarship. But what's wrong with us? Why does he have to leave us?"

"Won't he tell you anything?"

"He shuts up like a clam if I say one word about it. 'You live your life,' he says, 'And I'll live mine.'"

"Remember how much fun last year was?" Corey asked as they headed to the gym.

"Not anymore. This year has blocked it out!"

Luke was already in the locker room, struggling with his lock. He had some kind of mental block about combination locks; it took him longer than anyone to get his open, and he had to carry the combination on a piece of paper because he kept forgetting it. He was whispering the numbers and directions to himself as he meticulously inched the dial around. Noah, whose locker was next to his, stood there snickering.

Luke and Corey made nervous eye contact and Corey slid off to his own locker. He changed into his practice uniform, listening absently to the talk around him.

"How you doing?" Antawn asked.

"Okay," Luke said. "Look, I'm sorry about Friday. I didn't play my best. Corey and I had a fight and we were both off."

"No problem," Antawn said mildly. "Noah, how you doing?"

Corey listened to see if Noah would answer. Antawn had a theory that racists these days made their point by just ignoring and refusing to talk to blacks. But Noah's answer was a gasp, followed by Antawn saying, "Oh, man!"

Corey turned around to see the three of them: Antawn, Noah, and Luke, all staring into Luke's locker like there was a horse's head in there.

"That's not mine," Luke said. He looked up at Antawn, pleading. "That's not mine."

Corey angled for a better view just as Landis came into the locker room. "How are you guys?..." and he saw the locker and froze, too.

In the bottom of Luke's locker was a dull-finished, big black handgun.

Corey's heart jumped around. His first thought was that Luke had flipped over the Claire incident and the gun was for him. He replayed the way Luke had said they should talk after practice, when everybody else was gone.

"Don't anybody move or touch it," Landis was saying. "Let me think."

There was nothing to think about. Bringing a handgun on campus was a felony. Landis was obligated to call the police. Luke would have an automatic three-month suspension and be barred from sports for the year. They had had lectures and orientation films on this stuff since their freshman year. Every time it was in the news that a kid brought a gun or knife to some other school, St. Philip would refresh everyone's memory about the rules and the consequences. They always said they didn't want to have to resort to metal detectors.

"What is that?" Noah asked Luke. "A nine millimeter?"

"How the hell would I know what it is?" Luke exploded. "It's not mine!" He turned to Landis now with the pleading eyes. "It's not mine."

As always, when in doubt, Landis looked at Corey. "Oh, my God!" he cried. "Look at you!"

Everyone turned from the handgun to Corey. He had forgotten the bruises. He had them covered up with a shirt at school today but in his jersey they were hanging out for everyone to see. Luke's fingerprints.

Luke's chest was going up and down. "Did I do that?"

Several other players had come in now and each froze in place, looking from Luke's gun to Corey's throat, like they were pieces of the same story. That's what the police would think, too.

"It's not mine!" Luke was turning from one teammate to the other, growing frantic. "It's not mine!"

"Luke, I have to call the police," Landis said softly.

"No!" Luke's eyes filled with tears. "Please. Just throw it away. It's not mine. Somebody put it there...." He turned to Noah. "*You* did this!"

Noah jumped back as Antawn and Ricky grabbed Luke. He fought them furiously. "I'll kill you!" he shrieked. "I'll KILL you!"

"Luke, shut up!" Corey wailed, aware that this whole

incident would have to now be part of the police investigation.

Noah backed up some more. "Get him away from that gun!" he said to Landis. "I don't want to be his next victim!" He looked at Corey significantly.

Landis was shaking. "Everybody please! Luke, calm down. You're making everything worse. Now... I've got to call the cops. I don't have a choice. If it's not your gun they can prove that."

"How do you know that?" Luke said, shaking off the guys who were restraining him. He pointed at Noah. "He's doing this! Can't anybody see that? He wants to play my position! He's doing this to me so he can play my position!"

"Oh, come on!" Noah scoffed. "What kind of smoke screen is that? What about the fact that you caught Corey with your girlfriend Friday night and tried to kill him? That sounds like a better motive than me trying to move up on the team."

Corey felt sick. Luke was screaming, Landis was dialing 911, the walls collapsed like pages in a kid's pop-up book and everything disappeared.

***

When he came to, Corey was lying on the shower floor, clothed but wet, and Antawn was standing over him. Out in the locker area, there were three cops; one putting the gun in a plastic bag, one writing down everybody's name, and one talking to Landis in his office. Luke was sitting on a tile bench, his hands cuffed behind his back, his head down.

"You okay? You fainted," Antawn asked. Corey nodded. "He's okay!" Antawn called out.

Corey got up. The pencil and pad cop—a young guy—was already walking toward him. "You're Corey Brennan?"

"Yes."

"How you feeling, pal? You feel like you could come out in the gym area and talk to me?"

"Let me dry off," Corey said. Antawn was already offering him a towel. "Why do I have to go out there?" Corey felt like he was being accused of something.

"They took us all out there one by one," Antawn told him.

"That way everyone can tell the story just the way they remember it," the young cop explained.

Corey thought that was a nice way to put it. He tried to stall for time. "Why does my friend have to be handcuffed?" he said.

The cop gently took Corey's towel away and steered him toward the door. "We'll talk about everything outside, buddy. Okay?"

"Okay." Corey twisted around, trying to make eye contact with Luke, but his head was down.

"I'm Officer Mercer," the cop said to Corey. "You sure you're okay? Don't feel faint anymore?"

"I'm fine. Is Luke under arrest?"

"Not yet. But we want him to come downtown and talk a little. Is he your friend?"

"My best friend. If he's not under arrest, why is he handcuffed like that?"

"He got a little excited while he was telling his story. It's for his own protection. Can I ask you some questions now?"

Corey blushed. "Sure."

The pad flipped open. "What happened in there?"

"Luke opened his locker and there was a gun inside. If he knew it was there, why would he open the door in front of everyone?"

Officer Mercer smiled. "Let's tell the story and work on theories later, okay, pal? Do you know Luke to own a gun? Or maybe his family?"

"No."

"Never seen him with one before? Does he ever talk about weapons? Read gun magazines?"

"No, nothing like that."

"What's wrong with your neck?"

Corey shivered. "Well...I'm sure somebody already told you. Luke did it, but..."

"He have a bad temper?"

"I don't know."

"He's your best friend, and you don't know his personality?"

"He loses his temper...but everybody does, don't they?"

"You and he been fighting over a girl?"

"No, sir. It was a misunderstanding. I broke up with my girlfriend Friday and Luke's girlfriend gave me a hug...like, because I was upset, and Luke got the wrong idea about it, you know?"

If Officer Mercer knew, he wasn't saying.

"When we're playing a game, sir, there's a lot of adrenaline."

"I'm sure that's true, but you don't see that many athletes choking each other at halftime."

"Officer, listen to me. I know this guy. This is a good guy. He would never carry a gun. I grew up with him. We go back—"

"Do you like him enough to cover up for him?"

Corey felt a jolt, like the officer had slapped him. "No!"

"How do you think that gun got in there?"

"Anybody could get in Luke's locker. He carries the combination around with him because he forgets it. He says it out loud when he's opening it. We've all told him that's not safe but..."

"Do you know anybody who would plant a gun in there?"

Say it! "It might be Noah Travers. He wants to play Luke's position on the team and he's new and...we don't know him."

The pencil was flying. "You think just to play a certain position, Noah would frame your friend for a felony crime?"

"I don't know but—"

"Maybe that's what you'd like to be true. You don't want to think your friend would get so angry at you. You must be pretty shook up after Friday."

"Noah...all I know is that Luke wouldn't bring a gun to school. I know that. I'd bet my life on it."

"Be careful what you're betting with!" The notebook, and, Corey thought, the mind, closed. "Anything else?"

"I guess not."

"Thanks buddy." Officer Mercer slapped Corey's shoulder and went back into the locker room. He and the other two officers—and Luke, still cuffed—came out. Luke looked at Corey with an unreadable expression. The door made a horrible sound, like a jailhouse door, when they went out. It echoed all though the gym.

Landis and the others drifted out, looking like zombies. "No practice today," Landis said. "We'll try and pick it up tomorrow, I guess."

They dispersed, except for Corey and Noah. "You need a ride home?" Noah asked Corey.

Corey shook his head no. He watched Noah walk away. The first thing Landis had ever taught them was to study the opponent and learn from them. Imitate their strengths and exploit their weaknesses. Corey knew he'd been at a disadvantage for three weeks because he hadn't understood Noah's game. But now he thought he did. He just hoped he had enough time to even the score.

Chapter

Sun-Sentinel

PHYSICIAN, HEAL THYSELF

Some columns, you really don't want to write. This is one of them. It's no secret I had high hopes for St. Philip's Badgers this season. I've been watching these seniors since they were freshmen; Corey Brennan, Luke Zabinski, Theo Stone, Antawn Lewis. They were a perfectly balanced team, all four making varsity in their junior year and almost taking St. Philip all the way. I knew this year, Gregory Landis was going to hold his first all-city trophy. I thought nothing could stop this remarkable squad.

I was wrong. Only two weeks into the season and the Badgers have succumbed to the most dangerous opponent of all—the enemy within.

Luke "The Physician" Zabinski, the Badgers' star center, was removed from school grounds yesterday and taken to police headquarters for questioning in connection with a handgun reportedly found in his locker. (See BOY, Sec. 2, p. 1.) Although no charges have been filed, this culminates two weeks of events that indicate the Badgers are on a path of self-destruction.

How it all adds up is unclear. No one will talk on the record about Zabinski's mysterious collapse at the season opener, or Theo Stone's abrupt withdrawal from the team, or the rumors that there was a fist fight at half time during last week's game with Dillard. How these things might be connected to the discovery of the gun is anybody's guess, but this many disasters for a school with a spotless record have to be more than coincidence.

If charged with the felony of bringing a gun on campus, "The Physician" could be looking at some hard time, especially if tried as an adult. To say nothing of affecting the lives and careers of all his teammates. Is a seriously disturbed boy being sheltered by a school that only cares about winning games? This is more than a wake-up call, St. Philip, this is a four-alarm fire.

Patti Starr

Corey's whole family froze in their places, in and around the kitchen, while he sat at the breakfast table, snuffling and chuffing and trying to stop crying as he read the column over and over. He'd been calm through the first article, on the front page of the Local section, titled, BOY QUESTIONED IN GUN INCIDENT. It was a short, straight piece, careful to say that Luke had been questioned and released, that no charges were filed at this time, but that police were still investigating. Then the article went on to list every kid in America who had shot someone or brought a gun to school in the past year, like Luke was part of some great conspiracy to destroy the world. No, worse than that, like all the high school kids of this generation were gun slingers and killers. It listed a number of video games and TV shows Corey had never heard of as the possible culprit.

Accompanying the article, like a bad joke, was Luke's junior prom picture—his grinning, dimpled, blond, scrubbed, Catholic-boy face looking moronically happy, like he didn't understand the seriousness of his crime.

All of that didn't break Corey down. It was Patti Starr, his favorite writer, who had given him his first ink when he was a "gifted freshman," a "shooter to watch." Now she was admitting she had the same hopes as Corey for the Badgers this year, but she was putting it all in past tense. He saw his scholarship, his whole future fading. He saw Luke in prison for something he didn't do. Jail. The crying jag hit him so fast and hard he couldn't even get up from the table and run to his room.

"Could you eat something?" Corey's mother asked. "How about a nice hot bowl of oatmeal?"

This was pretty lame since Corey's diaphragm was spasming so violently, anything he put down his throat would have hurled out his mouth like a cannonball, but he knew she was trying to help. "No thanks," he gagged.

"Maybe I can do something," said Corey's father, who was a lawyer. "You want me to call Luke's parents?"

"Thanks but...I don't think Luke wants anything from me at this point...." Corey held his breath as a new urge to cry took over. He'd tried to call Luke last night. Mrs. Zabinski had answered. She said Luke was there but didn't feel like talking. Corey had been planning to tell Luke everything about the Tylenol and his suspicions about Noah. He knew now he'd waited too long for that.

Renee brought Corey a handful of paper napkins. "But when he sees you at school today..."

Corey blew his nose. "He's suspended. I don't know when I'll get to see him." He took a deep ragged breath. The tears started to flow again.

His father put a hand on his shoulder. "Want to skip school today? It's okay."

Corey shook his head. "I have to go for the team. We have to try to—"

"Are you going to be able to hold up at my rehearsal Thursday?" Beth interrupted. "Because I'd rather you didn't go if you're going to be all messed up like this."

Both his parents started yelling at her then, which Corey was actually grateful for. All that sympathy was just making him feel sorry for himself. He knew he had to pull it together. People were counting on him.

***

After the initial release of emotion, Corey felt pretty good, pedaling his bike through a chilly October mist. He didn't drive today, because of what he planned to do tonight. He began to review his strategy, just like he would run plays in his mind for a game. Coach Landis had taught him a lot about defense—that you don't hurl yourself directly at a big, powerful opponent. "Never attack at a strong point," he had said. "Chip away at the weak spots, slowly crumble all the supports that hold the offense up. Then, when you're sure, you deliver your blow."

If Corey's thoughts over the past twenty-four hours were correct, Noah Travers was pure evil. He was possibly behind every bad thing that had happened around Corey for the past month. If that was true, he was much too strong now for a frontal attack. Step one was to find the weakest of Noah's weak points and begin chipping away.

Franny was standing in a little knot of cheerleaders and wannabe cheerleaders, stroking her own hair. As Corey approached, he could hear them gossiping about Luke. He tried not to get sidetracked by how angry that made him.

"He always looked dangerous to me...." Franny was saying. "Did you know he beat Corey up in the middle of the Dillard—" and here she broke off because her cortege had seen him coming and sent her eye signals to shut up.

"Hi, ladies." Corey tried to look like his old innocuous self, not a man on a mission. "Fran? Can I talk to you for a second?"

She eyed her friends, looking for nonverbal advice. Women were pack animals, Corey had learned long ago. They never made even the most personal of decisions without consulting the group.

"It's private," he said. "And it's really important."

"Is it about Luke?" she asked. "Do you know something?"

"It's private, Fran. Okay?" He turned and walked away, knowing her curiosity would force her to follow.

She trotted beside him. "If this is about getting back together..."

"It's not." He found a fairly secluded section of the schoolyard and faced her.

"Did you see the paper this morning?" She looked up into his eyes with her lovely green ones. "This must be awful for you."

Don't get sidetracked. "It's worse for Luke than for me," he said.

"What do you think he was doing with that thing?"

Don't answer that. "Franny, I want to talk about something else."

The long, black lashes swept down, then up. "Okay."

He cleared his throat. "I know all about you and Noah."

The blood rushed to her cheeks. "What are you talking about?"

Direct hit. "I know all about it. And I'm okay with it. That's what I wanted to tell you. You guys don't have to hide it from me anymore." He swallowed hard and added, "You're both my friends."

She frowned. "How did you find out? Did Noah tell you?"

He had considered saying that, to flush her out more easily, but he had realized that would leave him open to suspicion later. "I just found out, okay? It's not important how I know. I just wanted to say I'm okay with it. We were played out anyway, right? Don't you think?"

She lowered the lashes again. "Yeah."

"Noah's a great guy," Corey said. "I really like him." He casually touched his nose. It hadn't grown.

Franny put her hand to her heart and exhaled deeply. "Oh, what a relief. I'm so glad you're being like this. You're such a good sport, Corey."

"Yeah."

"Do you want me to fix you up? I know at least four girls who would love to—"

"No thanks. I like to do my own hunting."

She laughed. "You're the best, Corey. Come here, honey." She pulled him into a kiss, not quite like when they were dating, but close. Then she trotted off to tell her girlfriends.

Two points, Corey thought.

***

When he walked into the locker room, deliberately late, most of the team was already there: changing, tying up their shoes, stretching their hamstrings. He noticed there had been none of the usual talking and laughing and all their faces turned to him when he came in. All with the same look—lost, pleading, expecting Corey to give them their next cue. He realized the team captain was more important in a moment like this than the coach. He also noticed the only person who wasn't looking up was Noah.

"The only thing we can do for Luke now," Corey said quietly, "is to find some way to hold it together so he's got a winning team to come back to. Because he will be back." He looked directly at Noah when he said this, but Noah was putting great effort into lacing up his shoes.

Antawn applauded this, and the others joined in. "A-men!" he said. "Oh, and by the way, Corey, how the hell we gonna do that?"

They all laughed at that—the hysterical laughter of mourners after a funeral. Landis came in, looking old and... faded somehow. There was something dead in his eyes. He'd worked with Luke for four years. Corey knew this whole thing was killing him.

Without being told, they began setting up their folding chairs. The whole roster, for the third time in three weeks, had to be changed again. Corey really knew Landis was depressed when he failed to wheel his blackboard over. He just stood in front of them, clipboard over his stomach, shoulders at half mast. "You kids have had a lot of stuff come at you all at once," he began. "More than you should have had. You all know I've warned you about times like this—when your emotions get all kicked up—how you can't afford to let that affect your play."

This would have been more effective, Corey thought, if it weren't coming from a hollow-eyed man who looked like he was about to cry.

"If we go speculating, dwelling on what's happened, that will defeat us. We don't know why Theo left. We don't know why this thing has happened to Luke, or what it means. But the important thing is not to get caught up in it, not let it drag us down."

He seemed to hesitate now, as if unsure of what to say next. He pulled a stool over and sat on it, looking into each boy's face in turn before he spoke. "I know Luke didn't do this," he said. "He couldn't have. And they'll prove that. But here's the thing. If we go theorizing and speculating and doubting each other—do you see? It will tear us apart. We have to just move on."

"Maybe we should clear the air and tell what we think *did* happen!" Antawn said. He was bouncing in his seat, a bad sign. "And *then* we can move on!" He glared at Noah, who was still keeping his head down.

Corey touched Antawn's arm lightly. "No," he whispered.

Antawn shook him off as if his hand was a tarantula.

"That's a bad idea, Antawn," Landis said. "All we have left now is our team spirit." He had to pause, because Antawn had made a noise like a snorting horse. "What we need to do is make a good roster out of the excellent talent we have left. One good thing is that Noah can play center."

Antawn gave a little shriek and came up from his chair like a marionette in the hands of a bad puppeteer. "This is too much!"

Corey tried to pull him down. "Hey—"

"Don't you 'hey' me!" Antawn flung his arm in a wide arc. "You fool! Are you deaf, dumb, and blind? This is like *Murder, She Wrote*, man! This...this...thing..." —he pointed at Noah— "...comes in here, and now the bodies are dropping like flies. My best friend—gone! Your best friend—gone! Who do you think is next, Corey? It's either me or you! And meanwhile, this...*redneck* is getting to play starting center. Don't you get it, Corey? Are you stupid?" He waved his arms to include them all. "Doesn't anybody get it?"

Corey jumped up. "Let me talk to Antawn for a minute," he said to Landis. "In private."

"I don't want to talk to you!" Antawn was raving now. "What I want to talk to you for?"

Corey took a risk and clamped his fingers hard on Antawn's arm. It was like grabbing a live wire. "Just five minutes," he said, using sheer size advantage to drag Antawn toward the door.

"This like Nazi Germany, man!" Antawn shrieked, making his feet slide on the floor like a stubborn toddler. "This like Selma, Alabama!"

Outside the door, Corey let go of Antawn's arm and ducked, which avoided him getting a punch in the mouth. "Hey!" Corey said, stepping back several feet. "Do you always have to go crazy at the wrong time?"

Antawn folded his arms and marched up and down, a

technique he used to dissipate what Landis called "negative energy." "This is a great time to go crazy!" he said. He stopped suddenly and got right in Corey's face. "What up with you, man? You don't care about Luke and Stonehenge? You stickin' together with the other Irish?"

Corey leaned back a little. "Yeah, that's it. Me and Noah want to make the whole team Irish."

"Then you're like Landis. You just want the trophy no matter what. Even if we have to reward that redneck pig for bumping off our best friends. Is that what kind of—"

"I want to take Noah out and you're messing it up for me." Corey talked right over him, hoping he could hear.

"Huh?" Antawn came to a complete stop and stood there, panting.

"What did you think?" Corey said. "I'm as close to Luke as you are to Theo. You think I don't know that big jerk planted the gun?"

"Well, then—"

"We can't prove anything. And if we come right out and accuse him now, it only does two things. One, it destroys what tiny little bit of team morale we have left and two, it tips him off so he can build his spiderweb even stronger. We're up against something diabolical here. We gotta run a play."

"Yeah..."

"We have, like, no cards against this guy. He's good at this devious stuff and we're not. The way I see it now, the only ace I have is that he trusts me and he thinks I'm naive and stupid. At least with that I can maybe draw him out, get something I can use. And look, he won't do anything else right now. He got what he wants, he's the starting center, so right now he's harmless like..."

"...a lion who just ate," Antawn nodded.

"You got it. So I want him to relax, let his guard down. I can't do that with you yelling 'redneck' and talking about Selma, Alabama. Right?"

Antawn rubbed his hand back and forth across his mouth. "I'm sorry, Corey. Did I blow it?"

"No, I don't think so. If we go in there now and it looks like I muzzled you, then Noah will really think I'm a great stooge. He'll trust me even more."

"Yeah...but how you gonna get the goods on him? He's slippery."

"I'll figure out a way. I want Luke and Theo back on the team and him off!"

Antawn laughed. "And get us our trophy, too, while you're wishin'."

"I'm gonna do that, too."

Antawn patted Corey's shoulder. "Hey, I'm sorry I went crazy. I'm impressed with you. You were always a good guy, but I didn't know you had any *cojones!* What can I do to help you?"

"Just go in there and be good."

Antawn hooked his arm around Corey's shoulder. "Got my halo on. But just one favor, Corey. If Noah goes down, let me be there to see it."

Corey grinned. "I'll do what I can."

***

Predictably, Noah waited for Corey after practice.

"Want a ride?" he asked, holding the door for Corey.

"I rode my bike. Good practice, Noah. I think we've still got a winning combination."

"Maybe better than before. Put your bike in my car. We'll get a Coke or something."

"Not tonight. I have someplace to go." *I'm on a case. Your case, you girl-stealing, friend-framing, team-destroying...*

"I wish I could do something for you, Corey. You did me a big favor keeping the lid on that little Dennis Rodman wannabe."

Corey shivered. That did sound like racism, but it was still kind of a line call. "You don't have to thank me for that. It's my job to keep the team together."

"What did you say to him, though? He was ready to kill me and he came back as meek as a lamb." This time, Corey heard it loud and clear, *thanks for getting the boy back in his place.*

"I told him I believed in you. Antawn and me go way back. I have a lot of credibility with him, with the whole team. They all know how I feel about Luke and that if I suspected you of doing anything to hurt him...well, you get the idea. But I know you're a decent guy, Noah. You're ambitious, but you'd never cheat your way in."

"That's right." Noah nodded. "You know, I've seen a lot of kids hang around that locker room who don't belong there. There's a bunch of Cubans..."

"The important thing is, I don't want the team to scapegoat you because things are going wrong. I know you a little better than some of the rest of them do. I know what kind of person you are. Antawn was just frustrated because…well, we all love Luke and Theo and we want somebody or something to blame."

Noah touched Corey's shoulder. "Well, thanks for believing in me. You don't know what that means. Anytime I can do a favor for you…"

They were at the bike rack now. Corey squatted to open his lock. "Actually, you already did me a favor, so we're even."

"I did you a favor? What was that?"

Corey straddled his bike. "I know about you and Fran McDermott. I've been trying to get that girl off my hands for the past year. Good luck!" He spun off with a cheery wave while Noah stared after him, forgetting to close his mouth.

Two easy skirmishes, Corey thought. He had established that Noah was a liar and a sneak, and he had proved to himself that he could fool Noah and jerk him around. But now, tonight, there was a real battle ahead, Corey thought as he picked up speed and merged into westbound traffic.

He knew he could never take Noah down until he understood exactly how Noah had accomplished all his dirty work. You can't defend against a play unless you know how it works. So the next stop was Theo Stone.

Chapter

Corey had only been to Theo's house a couple of times, but he remembered the way. He felt guilty that he was afraid to bring his car into this neighborhood, but he comforted himself with the thought that, in effect, he was probably sacrificing his bike.

Kids were out in all the yards and streets: some playing  ball, some doing nothing. The ones who did nothing were scary. All of them looked at Corey, not menacing, but curious, alert. He didn't belong there.

Theo lived in a small frame house, too close to its neighbors to have a decent yard. It was the gingerbready kind of house they built in Florida twenty years ago, before they realized wood was a bad idea. A worn-out, portable goal leaned against the side. There were wooden steps leading up to a tiny porch with a railing around it.

Corey walked his bike up the steps and leaned it against the house before knocking. At least he could minimize the risk.

Theo's grandmother, Gigi, answered the door. Corey remembered her from freshman and sophomore games, but there was something wrong with her legs and she couldn't navigate the bleachers anymore. No one ever asked, and Theo had never offered to tell, where his parents were.

"Corey? Is that you?" She peered through the screen door at him. She looked older than Corey's mental picture, but still beautiful with her peaceful eyes and her salt-and-pepper hair braided and coiled around her head. "Look at you, honey! You've shot up! How tall are you now? Come in." She held the door wide. "Do you want to bring your bicycle inside?" she added, glancing at it.

"No, it's okay." It was a point of honor now. "There's dirt on the wheels." He didn't know if he was supposed to answer all her questions or move on. "I'm six two now," he said. "Luke Zabinski is six six. We all grew."

"All except Antawn!" she laughed. "And he's the one I think is really going to the NBA if anybody does. Can you stay for supper, honey?"

There was a wonderful smell in the air. "No, they expect me back at home. I just wanted to talk to Theo for a second. Is he home?"

"He's in his room." She rolled her eyes. "Weight training. It's always something like that with you boys." She lowered her voice. "What is this business about Luke?"

"He didn't do it," Corey said. "He's a good guy."

She nodded. "Yes, I remember him. Do you know about Theo wanting to transfer to Northwest?" It seemed like she'd raised her voice a little for that, like she hoped Theo would hear. "Don't you think that's crazy?"

"Yes, I do," Corey said. "That's why I'm here. We need him. Do you have any idea why he'd do that?"

She sighed. "I wish I did know. I know he didn't always like to be in the Catholic school. I don't mean any offense. It's just that we're not Catholic."

"I know."

"But I wanted him to stay there, for the education. As good as he plays, he's a student, he needs to get in a good college and plan a real future. When they came to us from St. Philip and offered to pay his tuition, I thought that was like destiny calling."

"It's a great school." Corey had never known Theo was recruited. He didn't even know St. Philip did things like that.

"Well, maybe you can talk some sense into him." She picked up a cane and leaned on it, leading Corey down a small, dark hallway. "He's crazy to transfer now. He's played with you boys since you were freshman. He'll lose half his credits...he'll never get to the playoffs like he wanted to...."

"We might not either, without him," Corey said.

"Well,"—she pointed to a partially open door—"see what you can do." She slowly made her way back down the hall.

Even though the door was ajar, Corey tapped lightly before going in. Theo—a man too big for his room—was on his back on a battered, red vinyl bench with stuffing poking out of one side, pressing free weights. The only other things in the room were a narrow cast-iron cot that was at least four inches too short for Theo's legs, and a particle board dresser, the top of which was crammed with trophies and prizes and his freshman-year shoes, now several sizes too small. The space under the cot was apparently for books, which were spilling out on three sides. Where Corey's walls were hung with beautifully glass-framed NBA posters, Theo had pictures torn out of *Sports Illustrated* stuck up with tape. But the meaning was the same.

He pressed the weight with perfect form, no strain showing at all, except his dark skin was studded with beads of sweat that sparkled in the late-afternoon light like tiny diamonds.

He saw Corey, dropped the barbell a little too fast, sat up and wiped his face on a towel. "Oh, Christ!" he said.

"Listen to me," Corey began and felt himself nudged from behind. Gigi had maneuvered herself into the doorway.

"You boys want a Coca-Cola?" she asked Theo.

He slapped the towel down on the bench. "No!" he bellowed. "I'm not having a party here. What did you let him in here for? Don't you know a salesman at the door when you see one?"

Gigi sniffed and raised her chin. "I think maybe you need what he's selling!" She withdrew before he could answer.

Theo got up and shut the door. "Whatever you're going to say, it won't work."

"Can I sit down?" Corey sidled to the bed. "What are you pressing there? One-fifty?" He guessed low on purpose.

"One-fifty!" Theo growled. "Are you crazy? Gigi can lift one-fifty. I got two hundred on there. Oh, I see. We're starting out with flattery."

Corey laughed. "Right now I'm saying everything I can think of so you won't throw me out."

Theo relaxed and smiled. "How's Luke?"

"I don't know. He wouldn't come to the phone last night. Claire will hardly speak to me...."

"It's a mess," Theo concluded. "So Luke needs you, man. What are you doing at my house?"

"I want to ask you a question."

The huge arms folded. "You can ask it. I'm not gonna answer it."

Corey tried to stare him down, forward to guard. "I want you to tell me what Noah did to get you off the squad."

Theo had a good stare of his own. "No."

Corey paused, thinking. "If you say no, that means my premise is right. He did do something."

"No, it means I'm not talking to you and you ought to get out of here if that's all you came for."

This was precisely what made him such an excellent guard. His wall was always solid. No place to get a foothold. Corey wasn't done though. "If you don't help me, Luke could go to jail. You want that?"

Theo's eyes flicked away, then back. Corey went for a drive. "I'm gonna get him, Stonehenge, with your help or without it. He's hurt my favorite person in this world. He's killing my team. He's screwing up everything I ever cared about. I'm not going to sit by and let him do it without a fight. If you help me, I might go into this smart and make the right moves. If you don't help me, I'll go in stupid and do my best and maybe I'll be the next victim. It's up to you, but the part about trying to get him—I'm gonna do that either way."

Theo closed his eyes. He shook his head like someone arguing with interior voices. When the eyes opened again, they were shiny with tears. "I can't. If you knew my story, you'd understand why I can't. I love you guys. I love St. Phil. I thought it was a stupid school at first, all the saints and martyrs and whatever, but you're my team now. You're my home team. I'll be a stranger at some other school. You think I'm not angry that he's pushing me off my turf? It's not his school. It's mine!" His eyes flashed, but then went dull again. "But I can't help you, Corey. I just can't."

Gigi pushed her head in the door again. "You sure you

boys don't want a Coca-Cola?"

Theo raised his head and roared. "Do you have stock in the Coca-Cola company?"

She pulled herself up very straight. "What did you say?"

Theo giggled and ducked his head like a little boy. "I'm sorry, Gigi. It's your timing, was all."

"Showing common courtesy has nothing to do with timing. You do it *all* the time."

"Yes, ma'am."

"And especially to your elders when all they want to do is offer you a nice Coca-Cola." She was trying not to laugh.

So was Theo. "A nice Coca-Cola. You're right. Thank you, but no, my friend and I do not care for any refreshments at this time. If it so pleases you, wise elder and queen."

She chuckled. "I liked that. That was pretty good." She disappeared again.

Theo smiled after her. "She's an angel."

"Yeah." The interruption had helped Corey. He had time to see what was wrong with his strategy. Instead of going for the big question, he'd break Theo down with little questions. *Chip away.* "Do you think Noah put that gun in Luke's locker?"

"You know he did!"

"And he did something to you, too, didn't he? You don't have to tell me what, but I know you wouldn't leave a good school and a winning team and all your friends unless he brought out some heavy stuff against you. Am I right?"

"Look, you know this much. Why do you have to—"

"I've ruled out the possibility that he physically intimidated you," Corey grinned.

Theo guffawed.

"And he didn't set you up like he did Luke. He did something sneaky, something private."

Theo held up one hand. "Okay, you're out of bounds again."

"It has to be either bribery or blackmail," Corey pressed on. "And since I don't see you driving a Jaguar to school..."

"Come on, now..." A very threatening look. Corey kept in mind that he weighed less than what Theo could bench-press.

"He's blackmailing you, Stonehenge. He's got something on you."

Theo came up off the bench. "I said, that's enough!"

Corey's spine trembled. But he also thought Theo would never hurt him. He was willing to bet on that. "Don't let him get away with it. He's taking your future away from you! You want to go to a gang school and play for a losing team?"

"They're three and one this season!" Theo stood over Corey, but didn't look that threatening. "Better than you!"

"The season just started and you know it. They've got three big guards already. What are they gonna do with you? You'll be on the bench drinking Gatorade, buddy. How about that scout from Duke that writes you love letters every week? You want that to stop?"

Theo's shoulders sagged. "Damn you." He walked back to the weight bench and sat down heavily. "You think I need you to tell me I've been messed with? I know. I'm not as destroyed as Luke, but I'm semi-destroyed. But I'll tell you this much, *buddy*: If it got out? What he has on me? I would be as good as dead. This is what you need to know, Corey. However smart you think Noah is? However much credit you give him for plotting and scheming? He's way ahead. He's ahead of your worst nightmare. That's how good he is. He blindsided me so hard I saw stars! And that's really all. Okay?"

Corey was baffled. Theo didn't drink, smoke, or use drugs. He was a good student who wouldn't cheat on an exam if his life depended on it. If somebody dropped money on the sidewalk, Theo would run after him to give it back. He only dated girls in his church's youth group, and he hardly did that. When he came to school dances, he was the guy who would dance with all the fat girls and wallflowers so they wouldn't feel bad. What the hell could a guy like that do to get blackmailed for? "Does Antawn know about it? Whatever it is?"

"No! Now please leave me alone."

Antawn and Theo were like brothers. What could Noah find out that Theo had hidden from his best friend? "What are you?" Corey said, exasperated. "Gay?"

It was a long, horrible silence. Theo's eyes were unfocused, like a man in prison.

"No!" Corey said. "No!"

Theo kept on staring at nothing.

"But you can press two hundred pounds!" Corey wondered how many more stupid things he was going to blurt out.

Theo chuckled. "That's got nothing to do with it."

"Are you sure?" The stupid remarks weren't through yet.

"I'm as sure as I can be!"

"And you never told Antawn?"

Theo sat up and rubbed his hands over his face. "I should

have. I think he would have handled it okay. I guess I... didn't want to burden him."

"How did Noah find out?" Corey said. "Did he see you someplace...with somebody?" Corey really felt like a fool. He seemed incapable of saying anything intelligent.

"No." Theo's eyes were almost eager, like he wanted to talk about it now. "I made a decision...to be celibate for now. At least through high school, and I don't know about college yet. Because...well, you know how it is in sports...I didn't want to be harassed...."

"Sure. I know. But there're gay players in the NBA. There's—"

"I know it. But that's the NBA, not a Catholic high school in Nowhere, Florida. I know it sounds like I'm ashamed of who I am, but—"

"No, I understand. I'd do the same if it were me," Corey said. "Does Gigi know?"

"She knows. She goes with me to group therapy every week, a thing for teenagers and their parents. It meets at the library every Tuesday night. That's how I think Noah figured it out. Because he pulled me over on a Wednesday—I'll never forget it—and asked me how would I like to step down so he could get off the bench. He said, 'How would they like to know their two-guard is a—'"

"Don't." Corey held his hand up. "Don't quote him." Wheels were turning in Corey's head. "Do you realize what this means? He had to be following *all* of us around! Snooping around like some detective. That's the only way he'd know you have a meeting on Tuesday nights! He has to have been *following us all,* looking for weak spots!"

155

"And the weakest spot was me," Theo sighed.

"I think he has us all scouted!" Corey's mind was racing. "He took Franny away from me hoping maybe that would make Luke and me fight over Claire. He realized how lax Luke is about his locker combination.... This is beyond what a normal person would do! It's scary! Even a normally ambitious guy wouldn't plot and plan—"

"This is what I'm trying to tell you. Don't tangle with him, Corey. You don't have anything else he wants. You're safe."

"It's no wonder he got so far so fast. Nobody could have second-guessed him. This kind of—"

"'Evil' is the word I would pick."

Corey leaned forward, touching Theo's arm. "If I can get rid of him—take him out—and I promise you I'll never tell anyone your secret—would you come back on the squad?"

Theo's eyes said he wanted that. "You can't, Corey. Don't try. He's too good. He'll get wise and do something to hurt you. He's ten plays ahead of all of us."

Corey's fingers tightened. "But if. If I can beat him, neutralize him so he can't hurt you? Will you hold off your transfer? Will you just give me a couple of weeks?"

"A couple of weeks is a couple of games. I need to keep playing somewhere. I can't stay in my room trying to maintain my physique like a jailbird!"

"Two weeks. At the most. Please. I need you on my squad."

"You can win without me."

"I don't know if we can. And anyway...you and me and Luke and Antawn...we've been a team since we were freshmen. When we all went to varsity our junior year, everybody knew, Landis and everybody, that we would be a 'Dream Team' this year. That's the way I've always pictured it—the playoffs, the all-city, maybe even the state championship, but all four of us. Together. That's the way my dream *looks*. Some other way won't be any good."

"You sure? You want to risk everything to take on a madman?"

"For Luke I would. For you I would. Yes!"

Theo stared at him. Then slowly put his hand on top of Corey's. "I guess for that I could give anybody two weeks. Just remember…you don't know what he has on you."

"He already did his worst to me and I'm still here. He can't do anything to me."

"Don't say that, brother. This boy's in league with the Devil himself."

Corey got goosebumps. Not because Theo was scaring him, but because he'd called Corey brother. The black guys on the team never used that word except with each other. If they wanted to be affectionate with a white guy, they'd call him "man."

"Landis told me something about myself once," Corey said. "He said the reason I score so much is that I'd literally rather die than lose."

Theo let go of Corey's hand and sat back. "Tell me what I can do to help."

"Just give me two weeks before you do anything. Oh, and is there any way to get a Coca-Cola around here?"

***

Landis called for an extra practice every morning that week so the new lineup would be ready for the Nova Titans.

"We have to see ourselves in a completely new way," he said, banging his chalk against the board. "Before, we had a perfect balance of offense and defense. Now we're an offensive team. We need a different strategy."

Antawn slumped against Corey's shoulder. Morning practices were not his thing. Corey gave him a discreet elbow in the ribs.

"Offensively, we've got Corey and Noah and that's a lot." Landis drew two triangles on the board. None of the boys ever knew what these diagrams meant. "Corey's our go-to guy, let's say seventy percent of the time. We want to try and rack up a lot of points as fast as we can and depress the other guys into making mistakes. Corey, your job is to find your zone, get in close, and stay open. You don't have to worry about anything else, just shoot, shoot, shoot."

"Right." Corey thought he could hear Antawn snoring quietly.

"Everyone else's job is to protect Corey and get him the ball." He drew a line like a smile. "When Corey's in trouble, go to Noah 'cause he's almost as good."

Corey grinned, wondering what Noah thought of that!

"Noah, you're so good from the outside, I want you to just orbit the perimeter, stay way out. They won't know where to put their defense that way. Okay?"

"Got it," Noah said. He had his legs stretched out over three folding chairs, just to show off.

"Now, Antawn, you're going to be my wild card. Antawn?"

Antawn jerked upright. "Zone defense," he said, nodding.

Landis shook his head. "We were talking about offense, Antawn."

"Go to Corey," Antawn said.

Landis laughed. "Good guess. We're playing Corey inside and Noah mostly outside. I want you to be our secret weapon. While they try to pin down our two shooters, I want you to do what you do best, zigzag, steal the ball, and dunk it in there. You got it?"

"Corey inside, Noah outside, zigzag, steal, dunk," Antawn said.

"Good thing you're a quick study!" Landis said.

Antawn offered up a charming smile. "I like to learn fast and make time for my nap, Coach!"

"I'm gonna miss you next year, Antawn."

"Don't worry, I'm not doing so hot in math. Maybe I'll be back!"

"Can we talk about the defense, please?" Noah said.

Landis's smile faded. "Yeah, defense."

Corey echoed the sigh. Ricky and Tim were good players but they lacked experience.

"I want you guys to remember when the Bulls just had Jordan and Pippin, back in the eighties. Know what I mean? They had all shooting and no defense. But they won games."

"I remember," Antawn said. "And every year the Pistons plowed their asses!"

"Language, please!" Landis winced.

"Every year the Pistons brought them to grief."

"Well, that won't happen to us. Because all of you are

going to have to learn to play defense now. You don't have Theo watching your back. Noah, you're a great natural guard. A lot of the burden will fall on you. I do want a zone defense, and Noah, when somebody isn't covered or covered well, it's your job to take up the slack."

"I can do that." He yawned and cracked his knuckles.

You can do anything, can't you, Superman? Corey thought.

"Antawn, be aggressive, but count your fouls. If you foul out, we're in trouble defensively."

"The refs pick on me!"

"Okay, but just for an example, when you fouled out in the Dillard game, I personally observed you standing behind the man you were guarding with your arms around him, holding his jersey in both hands and it looked like your knee was going into his ass. Was that an unfair call?"

"Language, please!" Antawn said.

Landis turned to Corey, who got a sinking feeling. "Corey, it's time for you to learn how to guard. You realize that."

Corey squirmed. "Yeah, sure."

"No, I'm serious. You're used to being the star shooter, having great guards to back you up. You're big and strong and quick and I need you in both courts. You've always been a slacker on defense, but we can't afford it now."

Corey felt his face heat up. "I understand," he said.

"You can't stand there politely with your hand up like you're trying to get a taxi. You have to get in people's faces."

Corey breathed deeply so he wouldn't get mad. "I can do that."

"Show me you can. I'm sorry to harass you, but you've got a weak spot we can't afford right now. Nobody fears you. People shoot right through you, like you aren't there. You can't be a nice guy and win games."

Corey spoke through his teeth. "I understand what you're saying." He felt Antawn pressing his ribs, urging him not to lose it.

"The Titans want to violate your goal, Corey." Landis was pointing a finger at him now. Shaking it at him. "They want to take something that belongs to you. You gotta get mad and let them know they can't get into your goal. You gotta get furious."

"I *can* get mad!" Corey shouted. "You think I never get mad?"

"I think you're too polite to show it! I think you're going to lay down and get us raped with your Goddamn courtesy!"

Corey jumped up, feeling the undertow of Antawn grabbing his jersey. "Goddamn you!" he screamed at Landis. "You don't know me! You don't know what I can do if I'm at a wall! You talk to me like *I* would be the one to blow a championship? Me? Are you crazy? Nobody's gonna take anything from me and get away with it! You watch somebody try to shoot through me! I'll *kill* them!" He stopped suddenly because he heard himself, and the echoes of his screaming were truly terrible in the acoustics of the locker room. He also stopped because Landis was holding his hand out.

"I'm sorry, Corey. I was messing with you. I thought it was important for you to get to that feeling, so you could remember it when you need it."

Corey was panting. He waited for several more waves of anger to pass before he tried to speak. As his muscles slowly unclenched, he felt Antawn let go of him.

Everyone kept watching, to see what he'd say, what he'd do. He didn't glance at Noah. He realized his eyes were filling up with tears. "Thanks, Coach," he said and sat down.

Chapter

Fat, gray stormclouds hung over the city on Thursday—matching Corey's mood. This would be hard, and tonight was Beth's stupid rehearsal dinner. Corey drove to Luke's house on automatic pilot, rehearsing what he wanted to say.

The route was hard wired into Corey's brain. They'd been friends since third grade. Luke's home had always  been Corey's favorite place to be. He pulled into the driveway, parked, and got out of the car. He felt a weird stillness over the neighborhood. The wind came in cold, nagging gusts. It was like Luke's sadness had escaped from the house and poisoned the whole street.

In the past, he would have knocked. Today, for some reason, he rang the bell.

Luke's mom answered the door in a little pink sweatsuit. She was tiny, with little delicate bones, and a voice that chirped. Luke's tall genes had come from his father. The Zabinskis had raised five boys—two basketball players, two track stars, and a gymnast. Luke was the baby, and by the time he was in high school, Mrs. Zabinski had perfected her techniques. She always had the house stocked with food and soft drinks. She knew how to kid guys without embarrassing them, how to be friendly without getting in the way. She never gave you a look for putting your big feet on the coffee table and if she accidentally heard a belch or a four-letter word, she let it pass without a comment. She was the only mom who wanted the guys to come over. The others only tolerated it.

Today, looking into her alert, brown eyes, Corey realized he loved her. Whatever he was about to do would be for her, as well as for Luke.

"Oh, Corey, I'm glad you're here," she said, although her voice trembled a little. "Luke's in the backyard. He's been so depressed. I can't think of anything to cheer him up."

Corey tried not to smile. He could well imagine Mrs. Zabinski making French toast and offering to take Luke to the movies, as if that would take his mind off his life being destroyed. It was people like her that Noah hurt the most. People he didn't even know.

"I'll just go back there, then." Corey stumbled away.

"Okay." She started to close the door, then opened it again. "I saw the paper today. That was a nice quote you gave the reporter last night."

Corey waved his hand as if the praise were an insect that would sting him. "It was the only thing to do." He ducked his head and retreated.

Coming around the side of the house, Corey saw an image of Luke he knew would become a permanent photograph in his brain.

They had a big linden tree in the backyard with a tire swing Mr. Zabinski had put up fifteen years ago for Luke's oldest brother, Danny. The swing was on its third tire, and maybe the ninth or tenth rope. When they were little, Corey and Luke would use the swing to do wild, dangerous maneuvers: try to swing higher than the limb, jump out in midswing, imitate the two-man trapeze act they'd seen on TV. They'd had a club for a while where the initiation involved drinking rainwater from the tire. But since junior high, Corey and Luke had moved operations to the basketball goal, and the swing had hung there, unused.

But Luke was there now, not swinging but hanging, suspended by his waist, his long legs coming out of one side, his torso and arms arched backward to touch the ground on the other side. As Corey watched, Luke was slowly crabwalking in a circle to twist up the rope. When it was sufficiently bunched, he pulled his feet up and let himself spin, a blur with a recurring strobe of blond hair.

There was something so private about this, Corey hesitated to come forward, but standing there watching was worse. "Stop!" he called out. "You're making me puke!"

Luke twisted upright, unbalancing his rotation, dragging his feet, blushing. "Shoot," he said. Then added, "Hi."

"Hi." A horrible thing, feeling awkward with one's best friend. As Corey approached, Luke got out of the swing and sat on the ground, bracing his back against the tree. Corey slid into the swing, stretching his feet forward so they almost bumped Luke. "How are you doing?"

"Fine!" Luke said, raising his voice. "I'm fine!"

"Yeah, me too," Corey said. "I'm so happy, I can't stop crying."

Luke laughed a little, then said, "Good game last night."

He was going by the newspaper account. He hadn't come, as Corey had secretly wished he would. Corey gave Luke the same hand wave he'd given his mother. "Antawn carried the game last night. He played his little heart out."

Luke frowned at his lawn. "And you know, the other thing...what you said...that was nice."

"I just gave her the quote," Corey said. "The whole team wanted to dedicate the game to you."

Luke laughed. His eyes flashed up to meet Corey's. "Yeah, I bet it was real important to Noah to do that."

Corey had been rocking himself in the swing, but he stopped now. "I should have listened to you, Luke. I was wrong about him."

One corner of Luke's mouth twisted up. "I love being right."

"It's not over." Corey leaned forward. "He hasn't beat us yet."

Luke stared at Corey. The stormy day made his blue eyes look gray. "Speak for yourself."

"We can't let him get away with this. He blackmailed Stonehenge—"

"You don't *know* that."

"Yes, I do. I talked to him."

"Blackmailed him with what?"

"I can't tell you. But that's what he did. He had something on him and he used it. And he framed you."

"Yes, I know. But we can't prove that. I told the cops what I thought had happened. But they have to have proof."

Corey hesitated. He wasn't ready to make a full confession yet. "What about you? What's going on?"

"They don't know what to do. Whether they want to prosecute me or not. I got the feeling some of them believe me and some don't, or maybe they were all just acting, I don't know. We had a real frank talk down there at the cop shop. Corey—don't ever commit a crime. I've spent a total of six hours in that place and believe me, I'm scared straight for life. They're dragging people around the halls in shackles and stuff! And everybody has hollow eyes like pod people!" Luke was staring off into space as he remembered this. Then he looked at Corey again. His voice lifted an octave. "If this goes wrong and I end up in a place like that, I'll kill myself! I swear I will!"

"Stop that!" Corey put out his hand to steady the space between them. "You're innocent. They can't convict you of something you didn't do."

Luke took a deep breath. "They told me some of the stuff didn't add up. That's why they haven't charged me yet."

"Like what?"

"Number one, I opened up the locker in front of all you guys, like I didn't know what was there. Number two, they have statements from all you guys, except Noah, saying I looked genuinely shocked."

"What did Noah say?"

"He said my expression was 'hard to read.' Creep."

"Creep," Corey agreed.

"But that turned out to help me. They thought it was interesting he had a different spin from everyone else. That actually made them take me seriously. And then the big thing is that the gun was apparently wiped down."

Corey frowned, not understanding.

"There were no fingerprints on it. The cops said that was more the action of a framer than a guy bringing a weapon to school."

"So are they going to arrest him?"

"No. It's, like, just enough evidence to confuse them, but not enough to get him. They requestioned me yesterday and they said they had requestioned him and looked into his school records and stuff back in Georgia. They wouldn't tell me what they got from that, but it wasn't enough to tip the scales. They told me it would take a lot of evidence to shift an investigation to some other person, just because I say so."

Not yet. "Can't they trace the gun?"

"They did. That's what we talked about on my second visit downtown." Luke's gaze was drifting off again. He clearly didn't like his memory of the police station. His eyes locked on Corey, wild again. "Corey, this stuff is *killing* my mom!"

Corey wished Luke would stop saying "killing." "What about the gun?"

"It was stolen in a home invasion in Coconut Grove last summer."

Corey's whole body jolted. "Noah robbed a house in Coconut Grove?"

Luke broke into a laugh, the first genuinely happy laugh Corey had heard in a long time. "No, you moron! The punks who rob the house sell it on the street so they won't get caught. I guess if you want a gun, you just put the word out and it's like drugs, the sellers find you."

The wind was picking up, ruffling the leaves above them. Corey was getting a headache. "Noah knows how to buy a gun on the street?"

"It would appear so."

Corey took a long, deep breath. "Every time I think I have a fix on how evil this guy is, I find out there's more. I know from Theo that he probably stalked each and every one of us looking for stuff he could use. Now you tell me he's not scared to go into Miami and buy a gun off a criminal! Like, what else has he done? What else can he do?"

"I don't think he was ever arrested for anything. If he was, the cops would be taking my story more seriously."

"No, he's never been arrested!" Corey heard his own raving voice. "He's too smart for that! He's Superman!"

"Do you think Stonehenge would go to the police and tell them what Noah did to him?" Luke's eyes pleaded with Corey.

"He can't. Let that drop. He really can't."

"Then I don't see what else we can do but just wait to see if they think they have enough evidence to charge me." Luke pulled up a handful of grass.

Now. "There's at least one more thing we can tell the police." Corey looked down at his lap.

He felt his leg grabbed. "What?"

Corey closed his eyes tightly.

His leg was shaken. "What? For God's sake, I'm fighting for my life here! What have you got?"

Gently, Corey pulled his leg free. "This is going to be hard for me to tell you." He already felt tears stinging his eyes as he looked up at Luke again.

Luke sat back on his heels. "Okay."

Corey swallowed. And again. "The night you collapsed? The night I gave you the Tylenol?"

Slowly, Luke's hand came up to his mouth. "Oh, no."

"Noah gave me that bottle of pills."

"Oh, NO! No, Corey. NO!" Luke was getting up.

Corey braced himself. *If he hits me, I deserve it.*

Luke grabbed Corey's shoulder and shook it. "Why didn't you *tell* me? You gave me pills that came from him and you said they were yours? Why would you do that? What's wrong with you?"

"Ouch!" Corey knew he was going to have bruises from that grip. "I was stupid! I trusted him! I thought you were paranoid and I wanted you to take some Tylenol so you'd be a hundred percent for the game."

"Damn it, Corey!" Luke released his grip with a shove that made the swing rock. He turned away and paced, apparently trying to work off the desire to beat the crap out of Corey. "Who the hell are *you* to decide anything? I don't have a right to know I'm getting pills from someone I don't trust? That's wrong, Corey! That's just plain wrong!"

"I know." Tears were streaming down Corey's face now, but Luke didn't see it because he was pacing around.

"Suppose he'd wanted to *murder* me instead of just knocking me out? Or what if he'd decided to give me acid and make me go out of my mind?" He whirled on Corey. "I'd NEVER do this to you!"

"I know!" It came out a sob.

Finally seeing him, Luke pulled back in horror. "Don't do *that*!"

"Too late," Corey hiccuped. He covered his face with his hands.

"It's not fair to do that when I'm yelling at you!" Luke yelled. "Cut it out!"

"Just GIVE me a minute!" Corey yelled back. Then the absurdity of their whole exchange struck and he laughed in the middle of crying, which gave him the edge he needed to stop. He looked up and saw Luke had walked to his side and was standing very close to him. Not for comfort, Corey realized, but to shield the view of Corey crying from anyone looking out the back windows of the house.

Luke's anger had clearly been derailed. He looked like he was going to laugh too. "Better now, hon?" he asked snickering.

"Shut up." Corey lifted the hem of his shirt and wiped his whole face.

Luke assumed a campy voice. "This is just how Claire gets the upper hand with me!"

"Shut up!" Corey laughed.

"This could be a motivational tool, Corey. You could tell the team, 'you guys score right now or I'm going to cry!'"

"Shut UP!" Corey shoved him. "Sit down. I want to tell you something." Corey waited until Luke was a safe distance away. "Everything you just said to me was true. It's worse than what you said. The bad things that have happened to you and Theo are my fault. I let him get a foothold, I helped him every step of the way. If you'd known they were his pills, you wouldn't have taken them—"

"Got that right!"

"And even after it happened—I had suspicions then, but I didn't tell you. If I had, maybe we could have worked together, stopped him from doing anything else...."

"Why didn't you? I'm not trying to upset you again, but I really need to know."

Corey sighed. "I don't know if I know, Luke. I...before all this happened...my whole life, really, I've just always believed the best about people—and it's always worked until now. Most people aren't out to screw you. You treat them right, they treat you right. Maybe I just haven't been screwed over enough in my life to know…."

"Well, you're catching up now, Captain."

"But this is the thing, Luke. I was hanging onto my belief even after I knew it was wrong. Partly because I was greedy. Noah's a great shooter and I wanted that all-city so much. I just didn't want to look at what was right in front of me. But I hurt you, and I hurt Theo. There was a whole lot more to being a team captain than I ever thought."

Luke nodded. He always blew up in a very big way, but he forgave immediately. "Sure," he said. Thunder rumbled in the distance. Luke slapped at Corey's leg. "Don't feel bad. You did the best you could at the time. Your real trouble is that you're such a nice guy, you can't imagine how bad guys think."

Corey figured while he was getting absolution, they might as well go over all his sins. "Have you talked to Claire?"

Luke stiffened. "A little. I guess I should apologize to you. She told me she was coming on to you and you were telling her to stop when I came in."

"She's a good person, Luke. Don't let this mess you guys up."

He shrugged. "I don't know how I feel about that. I've got too many other problems right now."

"So let's work on them. Let's go to the police right now and I'll tell my story and at least they'll have another reason to question him again."

Luke shrugged. "It shows he's out to get me, maybe, but…do you have the pills?"

"They disappeared."

"They're just going to say you're my friend and you're lying for me at this point. You know? Because it's too late to say, 'Oh, wow! I remember another bad thing about Noah.'"

"I know that." A bright bolt of lightning tore at the sky. "Yikes!"

"We'd better go in the house," Luke said.

"No, we're going downtown."

"Corey, you don't have to martyr yourself. What you have to tell them won't really help me that much, and I think you're just trying to do penance at this point."

Thunder rumbled loudly. They both stopped to listen to it.

"I am trying to do penance," Corey said. "But I don't just want to tell them my little pill story. I'm going to make this whole thing right."

"Uh-oh, here's the God complex again. That's how we got into this mess!"

"You work with the tools you have. Go tell your mom we're going for a drive." Corey felt a few raindrops on his face.

Luke started to walk, then stopped. "Cor, I really don't want to go back to that awful place if there's no point…."

"You can go with me or I'll go alone!" Corey said.

Luke heaved a sigh and slouched off to the back door. The wind blew harder and the rain began to fall freely on Corey, running down his arms and into the collar of his shirt. This was always the point in the game where he felt the strongest. When the team was losing and everything was up to him.

***

"Here comes the bride! Dumb, fat, and wide!" Renee sang softly, then exploded into muffled giggles. She and Corey sat in the back of St. Philip's Church, which was shadowy and cavernous. Father Handrahan had only turned on the lights he felt were absolutely necessary.

Up at the altar were Beth, wearing jeans that made her butt look big, and Don, wearing khaki shorts worthy of a cane cutter. Only Father Handrahan was in uniform, boring everyone to death, intoning long passages about what God would do to Beth and Don if they entered into marriage lightly.

Up in front were all four parents and the small number of relatives Corey's father was willing to buy this extra dinner for. He had been delighted that most of Don's family and friends weren't flying in until the day of the wedding.

Corey and Renee had chosen to witness this solemn occasion from the rear of the church, and the family had not objected. It was the equivalent of the children's table at a family dinner.

"Here comes the bride," Corey giggle-hummed. "Bound, gagged, and tied." This evening was a tremendous relief to him after the horrible pressure of the afternoon.

"Broiled, stewed, and fried," Renee responded.

"Plucked, tweezed, and dyed."

"Fresh out of pride!"

"Sauce on the side."

"Groom better hide!"

Corey's giggling was getting out of hand. "What can we

do with astride?" he whispered, which made Renee collapse against his shoulder in helpless laughter.

Their echoes had obviously traveled up the nave. Corey looked up to see his mother on her feet, hands on hips, glaring back at them. All the proceedings had come to a grinding halt. The worst stares came from Corey's aunts, his mother's three sisters, whose dyed hair represented all the colors of autumn leaves. They believed Corey's parents were poor disciplinarians and often said so, which had the effect of turning Corey's mom, usually a perfectly pleasant person, into a commando whenever the family was around.

"What on earth is happening back there!" she shrieked.

"Sorry!" Corey called quickly. He was always the spokesman in any group of kids. Everyone glared at them a little longer, and then they all seemed to swivel around in eerie synchronicity.

"Why do they even have to rehearse a wedding?" Renee whispered. "The whole ceremony is 'repeat after me.' It's not like they're up there learning lines."

"It's just an excuse to have another family event and torture everybody," Corey said. "But just think. In one week she'll be gone. The house will be ours."

"Yeah," Renee sighed, "and in one year you'll be gone, too, and I'll finally be the only child I've always dreamed of being!"

"It will break your heart the day I leave home," Corey said, knowing this was true.

"Where were you this afternoon, anyway?" she asked, rifling in her purse.

"With Luke." He tried to sound casual.

She looked up. "How's he doing?"

"He's okay."

"What did you guys do?"

Corey told himself this only sounded like interrogation because he had a guilty conscience. "We just went downtown and messed around. Where were *you* this afternoon?"

"Went to a friend's house."

Renee was never vague like that. She loved to tell everyone the details of her life. "What friend?"

She was blushing! "Just a friend."

Disturbing as this was, it had shifted the focus off Corey. "Apparently a friend of the boy persuasion!"

She pushed him gently. "So?"

"So, that's new. My baby sister is growing up. It means someday you'll be up in front of a church in unflattering jeans. I need a minute to adjust."

"He's just a friend. Don't make a big deal out of it."

"That means don't tell Mom and Dad?"

"Right." She laughed. "It doesn't really freak you out, does it?"

It did, but why should that be her problem? "Hey, I'd rather see you hanging out with real live boys than talking to those wacky goths on the Internet."

She sat back and smiled to herself. Then she turned to Corey again. "Downtown? What's there to do downtown?"

He looked at her a long time. "Maybe this is the wrong night for us to ask each other a lot of questions."

She bit her lip. "You're right."

Chapter

Corey sat by the phone, resting one hand on the leg that was trembling. The morning paper was spread out in front of him open to Patti Starr's column. He had sent Renee off to run by herself. Beth and his mother were getting their nails done. His father was running last minute wedding errands.

Corey was prepared to call Noah, if necessary, but  everything would go down so much better if Noah called him.

It was nine o'clock. He wanted everything in place by ten. Noah usually called between nine and nine-thirty, but last week he'd waited till ten to call,
maybe because he'd figured out Corey's running schedule. Ten would be pushing it. Andrea Gemelli had to have her kid at soccer by eleven. They could do it without her, but...

Corey was getting annoyed by his own ruminations. *How do you tell your own head to shut up? Okay, if he doesn't call by nine-thirty, I'll call him.* He heard Landis's voice in his head, *Don't overtrain. You have to respond to situations fluidly.*

The telephone bell set off violent spasms in Corey's blood. It felt like the phone was ringing in his arms and legs. "Jesus!" he screamed. Then he let the phone ring two more times while he calmed down and scolded himself for being so jumpy. If he'd tried to play a game in this mental state, he knew it would go down the drain. He took a few deep breaths and when everything felt steady—five rings—he picked up, praying for a normal voice. "Hello?"

"Hey." Noah's voice was offhand—his usual prelude to asking for something.

"Hey yourself!" Corey said. "Did you see Patti Starr's column this morning? Now you're a freakin' miracle worker!"

Patti Starr had started her column with an update on Luke—he had been questioned twice, no charges yet filed, maybe something fishy about the evidence. Then she had gone on to say it was nothing short of a miracle that Noah had come along when he did, because the team had "barely missed" Luke's shooting and strategic skills with a center like Noah. Although Corey had cringed for Luke when he read it, he also knew it was a perfect setup for today. Noah would be feeling cocky.

"Yeah, I saw it," Noah said. Corey pictured him putting his feet up on something, blowing out his chest like a pigeon.

"Man!" Corey said. "It used to be me getting all the ink. Now it's you."

"It was a boring game," Noah said. "Those guys at Holy Cross play turtle ball."

Which was true. Antawn called them the Holy Cows. They just stood around, passing the ball like they wanted to be somewhere else. St. Philip had walloped them 72–32 and a lot of the 32 came from foul shots, because slow players drove Antawn crazy and made him too aggressive. He had fouled out in the third quarter on a technical. He'd started saying, "Moo" every time Holy Cross tried to shoot. Landis had argued weakly that "moo" wasn't a four-letter word, but the refs were mad by that time.

"Even so," Corey said to Noah, "you scored forty-four points and you drove that game. I was just like, your assistant." Corey noticed he was drawing a hangman's noose in the margin of the newspaper.

"Well, *thanks*!" Noah said. "Really, thanks. That means a lot coming from you. You know, from the day I tried out, Corey, all I wanted was to show you what I could do. Because I really respect you as a player. And a fair person. Not like those other creeps on the team. Especially the black guys. They hate my guts because I have an accent. I bet half of them think I planted that gun on Luke, just to get him out of the way."

Corey hadn't expected that. He hesitated, head spinning, deciding what to say. He settled on a noncommittal laugh.

"So..." said Noah, "you want to do something today?"

Thank you, God. "I don't know," Corey demurred. "I guess."

"Why don't we go to the gym and shoot hoops and then get something to eat? Or should I come over there instead?" Noah never included his own house as a possibility.

"My house is off-limits today," Corey said. "The wedding is tomorrow and all the females are in a frenzy."

Noah laughed. "So, I'll meet you at school. Like, eleven?"

"Ten would be better," Corey said. Held his breath.

"You got it. See you then."

Yeah, you big piece of... Corey hung up and did something he hadn't done in years. He prayed to St. Corentinus, his namesake, whom God had sustained with a miraculous, self-renewing fish. *Please help me reel this one in.*

Then he picked up the phone and started making calls,

putting his team in place.

***

Noah's black Nissan was already parked in the lot when Corey pulled in. Eager. Corey knew Noah had been trying to replace Luke in *every* way. That was something that could now be used.

From the doorway, he could hear the skid and thunk of Noah already practicing. He was magnificent to watch in action. His layups, regular and reverse, formed a perfect heart shape around the goal. When he leapt, his body tucked, leaving nothing for anyone to grab or foul. Corey would miss his talent on the team. "Hey!" he called above the racket of Noah's brilliance.

Noah executed a dunk, his only move that was a little awkward, came down unevenly on his feet and turned. "I'm all warmed up and ready to kill you, Brennan!" he called happily.

"I want to get something in my locker," Corey called, not breaking stride. "Come with."

Noah cocked his head. "I'll wait for you," he argued.

"No," Corey made an imperative sweep with his arm. "I want you to see something." He knew it would be a mistake to look back or slow down so he pushed through the door to the locker room, praying and praying under his breath.

There was a bad moment when nothing happened, then the door pushed open and Noah slid through, frowning. "What is this, Brennan? You got dirty pictures or something?"

Corey sat down on the tile bench and took a deep breath.

"I lied to you. I don't need anything in my locker. I want us to talk."

Noah slowed up. His chin lifted, like he was going to sniff the air. "Is this about your stupid girlfriend, Corey? Because I'm not even seeing her anymore."

"No, no." Corey gestured in the air, pressing something down with both hands. "It's nothing like that. I'm not mad at you. I just want to...say something...and then we can play. But it's on my mind and..."

Noah stayed in his frozen position. "Corey, if there's anything weird about you, just please don't go there, okay? I won't tell anybody, but please don't go there."

Corey laughed. "Noah. For Pete's sake! Are you scared to just talk to me? Why are you standing there like you want to run? It's like you've got something to hide."

That unstuck him. "Hide? What do you mean by that?" He took an aggressive step toward Corey.

"Sit down!" Corey said. "I need to say something and it won't be easy."

Noah sat very slowly on the opposite bench, eyes locked on Corey. "What?"

"You're probably gonna laugh at me," Corey began.

"Wanna bet? So far, this isn't real amusing."

Corey cleared his throat. "Okay, okay. Where do I start? Here's the thing, Noah. I've...learned a lot since you joined the team. I used to be—back when I hung out with Luke—like a choirboy, you know?"

Noah chuckled. "You got that right."

"Well..." Corey shifted like he felt uncomfortable. "I've been watching you, Noah, and I've been learning a lot about…ambition. I have as much ambition as you do, but I'm not as comfortable with it as you are."

"I'd agree with that."

Corey put his hands out. "I don't want anything to screw up my basketball career."

"Who does?"

Corey ran his hands through his hair. "I just…want to know if you're happy, Noah. Do you have everything you want? Because I don't want to miss something and end up…like Luke and Stonehenge."

Noah laughed again, a short explosion that jerked his body upright. "What the hell are you talking about, Corey?"

"It's okay. Believe me, I wouldn't say a word to anyone. I'm telling you, Noah. It's obvious to me what you did, and it's obvious what you can do, and I don't want…anything like that done to me, understand? So if you want to be team captain, or you want me to give quotes about you to the press…you want the ball more…I can make it happen. I can get Landis to do anything I say. Just tell me what you need to leave me alone and let me finish out this season and pick up my trophy. Okay?"

Noah was shaking his head back and forth, laughing and laughing. "Corey, you're mental. You think I *did* something to those guys to get them off the team? And now you're scared I'll use my powers against you? Is that it? This is too much."

Corey tried a voice that was higher, more childish. "Come on! I know what you did. With Theo. You were on the bench and you wanted to move to first string. You found out he was…vulnerable and you played a card."

"Vulnerable! That big tank? What are you talking about?

You think I'd target out a big muscle-bound—"

Corey interrupted what he was afraid might be a racial slur. "You know what I mean, Noah. I know about Stonehenge. I've always known about him."

Noah folded his arms. "What about him?"

"I'm not going to say it, just in case I'm wrong and you don't know. But the guy has a secret and I think you found out and threatened to make it public if he didn't get out of your way."

Noah was now smiling with his mouth, but frowning with his eyes. A very weird face to look at. "You're just sitting there calling me a blackmailer?"

"Come on, Noah. I know you think I'm like, from the farm, but I'm not that dumb. I'm the guy you gave the bogus Tylenol to, remember? What was in that, anyway? Don't you think from then on, I was looking at you differently?"

Noah cocked his head. "If you think I slipped something to your pal, why didn't you tell anybody?"

Corey paused. Lowered his head. Held his breath a little to make his face flush. Then he looked up again. "I've got a full scholarship to UM. My team is going to the playoffs. I want to get to my goals, Noah. That's why I'm talking to you right now and not somebody else. I'm telling you I know how...good you are at getting what you want and I'm trying to make sure *I'm* not in the way of anything you want. I don't know how to say it any clearer."

Noah was frowning, rocking himself slightly. "Corey! This is unexpected. Very unexpected. I *knew* you were one of those 'don't rock the boat' guys, but I never dreamed you were so weak and selfish you'd dump your buddies overboard like this just to stay on the boat yourself."

Corey held Noah's gaze. "I have a full scholarship at UM."

"Well, geez!" Noah said. "You seem to think I'm the Terminator or something."

"Two people have been terminated," Corey said quietly. "And I don't think the will of God did it."

Noah laughed and stretched himself. He was finally relaxed. "Brennan, Brennan, Brennan. This is great. You're more like me than I ever knew. It's just such a surprise that you could figure everything out like this all by yourself. I'm really, really impressed. So it was the Tylenol incident that sent you off on your detective career?"

"It was obvious. He took it, he went down. What were they? Were they Benadryl? I know he's allergic to that and you probably had that knowledge in your dossier somewhere."

"No, Sherlock. I didn't know that. It was Miltown. It's a tranquilizer my mom enjoys abusing. Two'll put you out. Zabinski did me a real favor by scarfing down three of them. That way I got to play the *whole* game." Noah looked as joyful as a child, remembering this.

"And you wonder why I'm afraid of you?" Corey asked.

"Come on, Brennan. You don't have to be afraid. You're my boy! You got me on the squad, took up for me whenever anybody said a bad word about me. Why would I want to do anything to you?"

"And it's true that you blackmailed Stonehenge, too, isn't it?"

Noah made a face. "Look, I did the squad a favor on that one. You want to be in the locker room with a guy that's checking you out?"

"That's stupid, Noah, and you know it. He's a great player and it hurt us to lose him." Corey hoped he wasn't saying too much, making anything obvious.

"He was a good guard," Noah agreed, snickering. "But now we know why. He liked grabbing other guys!"

"How did you find out about him?" Corey wanted to get the subject back where it belonged.

"Followed him around. He goes to some touchy-feely support group. God, I hate guys like that!"

"You followed him? Like a stalker? Until you found something?"

"That's right, choirboy. I did what I had to do. Lucky I found out about the group. I might have caught him doing something that would have given me nightmares for years."

Corey took a deep breath and let it out. "You must have followed us all around. You couldn't have known he'd be the one—"

"You make it sound more sinister than it is. It wasn't like a big project. You just pay attention. Ask questions. Do a drive by or two. If you're alert, you pick up things and then you think, how can I use this? If you'd put me on first string, I would have just filed that information and let it lay, but I needed it, and I used it." Noah was leaning back on his elbows now, in full brag mode. He was having a great time. It was safe to move in for the kill.

"And it was your gun, wasn't it, Noah?"

"My gun? You mean my gun, like something my Dad gave me for my birthday that I sleep with under my pillow every night?"

Corey pretended to laugh. "No, I mean your gun like you bought it somewhere and brought it to school and planted it in Luke's locker."

Noah smiled. "'Plant' is such a nasty word."

"I know it wasn't his. He's afraid of guns. Nobody else would have done this. You wanted to play center. You had his combination 'on file,' right? In case you needed it?"

"Well, the guy practically walks through the halls singing his numbers out. You can't help but hear him."

"Exactly! And you put the gun in there and waited for him to open it like a sucker."

"Look, Corey. I know you guys go way back. I don't want to say I did this and find myself lying on the floor with ice on my eye."

"We're not the same kind of friends we used to be," Corey said. "If I wanted to stick up for him, I would have done it when you drugged him, right?"

"You're very hard to figure out, Corey."

Corey pretended to get agitated, shifted his eyes around. "Look, he's a casualty, all right? I don't intend to go down with him. What have I been saying, Noah? I'm outclassed by a guy like you. I wouldn't know how to buy a handgun. I wouldn't know how to give somebody a pill to knock them out. I sure as hell wouldn't go to a guy who weighs 235 and try to blackmail him. The worst thing I've ever done in my life is lie in a confessional. Okay?"

Noah was chuckling through this whole speech.

"The only reason I'm trying to get this out in the open is because I want you to see, Noah. I know everything and I haven't ratted you out. I want you to spare me! I want to go to college and play ball and learn to be an English teacher so I can coach someday. And I want an all-city trophy so I won't *mind* being an English teacher, while Antawn ends up in the NBA. Okay?"

"Wild," Noah said. "Wild. Okay, okay. I want to help you calm down. Here's what I want. The next game we play, I want you to plant a quote on Patti Starr. Say I'm the backbone of the team."

"Backbone?"

"Or the linchpin, whatever. Just get that idea across. Say like, you don't know where the team would be without me. Something cool for my scrapbook. That's enough. I sure don't want to be captain and have to huddle with Landis all the time like you do."

Corey was pleased Noah had said that. "And then you'll leave me alone?"

Noah smiled. "I'll leave you alone. But I want a really good quote. You're a great talker. I have high expectations."

"Don't worry. Can I ask you a question?"

"Sure."

"If I had ever gotten in your way, do you know what you'd have done to me? Like, did you have something ready?"

Noah smiled. "You don't want to know, Corey. Are we ever gonna play ball?"

"Just one minute. One more question."

Noah sighed, but it was an egotistical sigh. He loved telling all this stuff, feeling powerful.

"How do you keep a straight face with the cops? I know they questioned you twice about the gun. How can you just lie to them like that?"

Noah grinned. "Lying is like breathing to me, Brennan. I've done it all my life. Half the time, I don't even know what's true myself. Now, can we play?"

"Let's play a different game now." A female voice rang off the shower tiles.

Noah started involuntarily and turned toward the showers where Andrea Gemelli, Officer Andrea Gemelli, was rounding the partition. She wore sweats today, her day off.

"You remember me, don't you, Noah? Corey told me he could get you to confess to everything and I didn't believe him, but I gave up part of my day off to see if he was right."

Noah looked like he was drugged. He turned his head, in slow motion, back to Corey. "No!" he said.

"Yes!" said Officer Gemelli. "And there's more. We've got lots of witnesses to call at your trial. Come on out, guys."

Antawn, Theo, and Luke filed out. Landis came last with an expression Corey had never seen before. He looked like he wanted to kill Noah.

"Bad boy, bad boy, whatcha gonna do?" Antawn sang.

"You're under arrest, Noah," Officer Gemelli said, stepping a little closer to him. "I'm really hurt that you wouldn't tell me all this stuff last week when I asked you so nicely."

"I was lying to him, showing off!" Noah said. "I made that stuff all up!"

She smiled. "You can say that at the trial if you want to. But all your friends here are gonna testify to what they think is true. You know how the jury system works, I'm sure."

Noah whirled on Theo. "You're going to testify? You're gonna go to court and tell everybody what you are?"

Theo showed no emotion. "I got to thinking, Noah. If I run from a dog like you, I'll be running from dogs all my life. I love basketball, but I don't have to play it. I can get into college on my brains. If scouts don't want me after they know who I am, so be it."

Antawn gave him a little slap of support. "Buy some cigarettes on the way downtown, man," he said to Noah. "You'll need 'em."

"Whatever happens to you legally..." Landis's voice came out almost a hiss. Corey had to look to make sure it was him speaking. "...you will never play on a team of mine again, and you will never attend St. Philip again. I already made sure of that."

"Don't worry, though," Luke chimed in. He'd been dying to speak. "Miraculously, I'm available to play your position."

Noah turned to Corey. His expression was more puzzled than anything. He drew in a very deep breath...too deep. It somehow looked wrong to Corey, not an inhale, but a body inflation, like a swan or a peacock or a cobra preparing to—

Noah sprang, sailing toward Corey in the tuck position, so Officer Gemelli's grab was useless. The image of a big cat flashed in Corey's mind just before impact. The back of his head hit the metal of a locker before he and Noah toppled onto the tile benches. Something in Corey's back went... pop! They all: Landis, the cop, the team, struggled to pull Noah off Corey. Officer Gemelli was saying something about "the hard way" as she wrestled her handcuffs out and pushed Noah down with her knee.

Corey was breathing through his mouth, each breath causing a ragged seesaw of pain somewhere in his side or back. He touched the back of his head and found blood.

Cuffed, Noah was still putting up a struggle, dragging Officer Gemelli and Luke around in a semicircle as he jockeyed to face Corey again, the whites showing all around his eyes. His voice was a growl, spraying saliva between his teeth. "I'm not done with you!"

Chapter

It was only nine o'clock and already the day seemed long. At five A.M., in the middle of Corey's third nightmare, Beth woke up the whole house by crying and wailing that she didn't want to get married, she didn't really know Don, her dreams would go down the drain when she started a family, etc. *What* dreams? Corey wondered. Other than wanting to

own a Porsche someday, he'd never heard of any ambitions on her part. As his parents quieted her down, Corey had rolled over and slipped into nightmare number four, in which Don turned into Noah and dragged Corey up the aisle to be a human sacrifice on the altar.

He woke up from that technicolor extravaganza at six-thirty and decided to stay up. He wished he could have had some downtime after yesterday. After Officer Gemelli had taken statements and dragged Noah off in the police car, Landis drove Corey to his second home, the emergency room, to make sure Noah hadn't broken Corey's back or scrambled his brains in the little skirmish they had. It was all good news; nothing but bruises, a slightly pulled shoulder and a small cut on his head that didn't even need stitches.

When he finally got home, there was a big crisis about champagne or something so Corey got away with saying he'd bumped heads with Luke while they were playing one-on-one. He planned to tell the whole Noah story eventually, but he didn't think anybody could absorb it until the wedding was over.

His father had given him a lecture about his lack of concentration, his mother had made a speech about how much she hated contact sports and then Beth had started whining that everyone was paying attention to Corey on the eve of her wedding and the discussion had flowed back toward the champagne.

After that, Corey had a bowl of soup and a hot bath and was just thinking about going to bed early when the phone rang—it was about eleven-thirty P.M. It was Noah's voice. "My mother is coming down to pick me up. Sleep tight."

Corey had slammed the phone down and it rang again immediately. He stood there shaking and after three rings, picked it up, afraid somebody else in the house would. "Best wishes to your sister tomorrow," Noah said.

"You've got the wrong number," Corey told him and hung up again. He had to sit down because his knees wouldn't hold him.

***

Now it was nine A.M. and there was so much wedding chaos that it helped Corey forget he was being stalked by a madman.

His mom was plugged into the kitchen wall phone talking to some aunt who was hung up in Raleigh and couldn't get a connector. Calls came in from Beth every five minutes. She and her bridesmaids were at the salon getting their hair piled up and it apparently wasn't working. "Sprigs!" Mrs.

Brennan shouted into the phone, presumably to the stylist. "It should almost be Japanese...no, I don't mean that at all!" She covered the receiver and turned to Corey. "I just know I'm going to have to go down there. How's your head?"

"Fine." He swirled the black sludge in the bottom of the coffee pot and ruled it out. "Where's Dad?"

"The caterer's. They've screwed everything up as well... Beth? I've got an incoming call, hold on...Hello? Don? What? Oh, *no*! Aunt Rose has the same problem. Yes, I know. Don, honey, why didn't you have them fly in last night? I know, but you...maybe Corey's basketball team could..." She glanced up because Corey was waving his arms like a traffic controller refusing a plane. "Yes, I'll call you back, sweetie—Beth? Are you there? Hold on, I have to do something, I'll call you back. Corey, come back here!"

Corey had almost made it to the door. "Mom, Beth only let me invite one friend. That means none of the team except Luke was invited. Now you're about to tell me that Don's goofy friends are stranded in Raleigh with Aunt Rose...."

"Honey, what else can we do?"

"It's rude to them! You're asking them to work when we didn't ask them to be guests!"

"But they're lovely boys. I'm sure Noah would..."

"Not Noah. And these guys have lives. I don't know what they're doing today."

"So call them."

"They don't have tuxes!" Corey was running out of stuff to say. He had never actually won an argument with his mother, but he always liked to try.

"They can pick up the ones they altered for Don's friends."

"No, Mom! Don's friends are probably a bunch of little chipmunks. My guys will burst the seams."

"Chipmunks" made her laugh, but she got right back on course. "Corey, listen to me. I have a caterer who is trying to bring Jewish food to a Catholic wedding reception. I have a daughter who says the stylist is making her look like a Geisha girl. I have a crying old aunt in an airport. All I'm asking you to do is get your friends on the phone and stuff them into some little tuxedos. Now go!"

Corey was laughing. "Yes, ma'am!"

On the way down to Renee's room, Corey wondered if he got his win-at-any-cost spirit from his mother. He'd never thought about it before. He knocked on Renee's door. "You up?"

"Yeah, why?" Tapping away as usual.

"Decent and all? I need to use your phone line for a wedding emergency."

"Come on in. You'll have to wait a minute. I'm answering an E-mail."

Corey came in and sighed at the sight of his baby sister in hot rollers and a short kimono, tapping out love messages to her microchip boyfriends. Where had his real sister gone? "The geisha girl look is bigger than I thought," he muttered.

"Huh?" Absorbed in her cyber-poetry. Corey angled around to try and see the screen.

"Wrap it up, sweetheart. There's an usher emergency...." He read the screen and stopped, startled.

"Hey!" She spun around and put her arm up.

Corey had seen the words, *just to say hello and give you a kiss, and then I have to...*

"I'm sorry!" he said, jumping back. "I didn't see a thing."

She frowned at him for several seconds to impress the lesson, then finished and sent her message. The next few years, Corey realized, were going to be hard for him.

"How's your head?" she asked, to make peace.

"It hurts if I touch it. I'm fine. In the kitchen, it's total chaos."

She smiled. "That's why I'm staying in here."

"Anyway, I have to call the guys to come and be ushers. Don's friends are stuck at the airport."

"Noah?" she asked. "Is he coming?"

"No, not Noah. He's busy today...the other guys." He didn't feel like bursting her entire bubble with everything else that was going on. "Anyway, you stick to the guys your age. You've got enough happening from the looks of it."

"You did read that! You big creep!" She stormed past him into her bathroom.

Corey sighed and sat down at her desk. Too much to think about today. He could hardly think straight. It was like when the other team made too many moves and his brain would flood and he'd do something incredibly stupid.

***

The church looked even more horrible than Corey had imagined it. There were pagan-looking bunches of corn, and wheat with colored ribbons weaving through them, and wreaths of dead sticks.

Grandma Monaghan was already in her seat, but she was always early for everything. Corey pulled his makeshift crew aside in the vestibule for a huddle. Corey and Antawn looked pretty good. Luke was showing a lot of wrist and ankle and Theo looked like he would come through his seams at any minute.

"Why'd she wanna do this scarecrow wedding?" Antawn screwed up his face. "If they put the priest in a hockey mask, you'd have the whole deal."

"Did you see the bridesmaids?" Theo asked him. "They look like yams!"

Corey waited for them to finish guffawing. "You better not laugh so hard," he said to Theo. "If you breathe wrong, those pants are gonna fly in every direction."

"Give the yam girls a treat!" Antawn said. "Corey, do you understand just how much this blows? I could be out satisfying my woman and here I am at a white hayride!"

Corey waited again. "Could you guys just listen to me for a second? I need to update you on the enemy."

"What?" Antawn got serious very fast. "He break out of the joint already?"

"I think he did. He called me last night and said his mother was on the way to get him. Maybe they released him to her custody or something."

"Aw, man!" Luke stomped his foot like a little kid.

Corey put a steadying hand on his arm. "And, he called me and said best wishes to Beth. So I'm scared the creep's gonna do something here to screw up the wedding."

"And here we are in a church full of straw!" Antawn said. "He's probably out there now with the gasoline can!"

"Let's call the cops," Theo said.

"We could try but they won't come," Corey said. "All he

said was best wishes to Beth. That's not a threat."

"It is if you watch TV," Antawn said grimly.

Luke was so mad his face was red. "How does he even know about the wedding?"

"Who knows?" Corey said. "He keeps a dossier on all of us. He probably wrote down important dates in there too."

"So what do you want us to do?" Antawn asked.

"Just watch the door, watch the parking lot," Corey said. "Any sign of him, grab him, hog-tie him, and bring him to me. He's got a black Nissan Sentra, but who knows? He might rent a limo and wear a disguise. Just shoot first and ask questions later, okay?"

"We'll take him out, Captain!" Antawn saluted Corey. "We'll throw holy water on him and he'll probably fry like an egg. Anything else?"

Corey looked out the door. The first cars were pulling up. "Bride's family on the left, groom's on the right."

***

The next few minutes were chaotic as aunts and uncles and weirdos and total strangers came pouring in, telling their life stories as the boys tried to hustle them to their seats and keep their eyes on the door. Don came in, pale and trembling, and Luke had to take him to a Sunday school room and let him lie on the floor. A call came from the beauty salon saying Beth's hair was still wrong and she'd be late. Dad arrived with Renee, who looked like a stranger in a pale yellow sleeveless dress and long earrings. It made him want to cry.

"What's holding up the show?" boomed a voice behind him. It was Great-Uncle Otho, famous for his big mouth. He waddled up to Corey and thrust his wrist in Corey's face. "It's half past two! Who's running this shoddy production! Elizabeth's not backing out, is she?"

"There was a hair emergency," Corey said, trying to demonstrate a quiet tone of voice. "She and Mom will be here any second."

But Great-Uncle Otho was apparently bored and didn't want to return to his seat. "Explain all these black ushers to me!" he boomed. "Is there a branch of the family I don't know about?"

The urge to cry came back. "It's my basketball team," Corey said. "My friends."

"Good God!" He waddled off.

Corey was considering going after him and saying something that would have his mother apologizing for years, until he saw a pale yellow dress slipping past him out the front door and everything suddenly clicked into place— too late.

All the circuits jammed in Corey's head, costing valuable time. *Just to say hello and give you a kiss, and then I have to...Best wishes to your sister tomorrow....* Renee's Internet boyfriend who turned into a real boy—how stupid could he be? Noah had come to his house, *seen* Renee had a crush on him, gone to her room, without including Corey, learned her E-mail address, and from then on Renee had been another item in the dossier. *You pay attention,* Noah had said. *Look for something you can use.*

Corey ran to the door and saw the black Nissan idling as

Renee strolled out to it. They called to each other like intimate friends.

"Renee!" Corey screamed. "Stop!"

Noah said something to her Corey couldn't hear. She glanced back and then continued toward the car. Corey charged, which made Noah jump out of the car, pull Renee in, and gun the motor. Corey ran to the car and pounded it. He was crying. "No, no, please!" he shrieked at Noah, who swerved to try to hit him as he screamed out of the lot.

Luke, the other guys, and most of the wedding guests were pouring out of the church. Corey half-ran, half-staggered toward his car. "Call 911," he yelled. "Somebody call 911."

***

Corey was doing about ninety on State Road Seven, swerving around traffic, trying to keep Noah in sight. Luke was in the passenger seat, talking to a 911 operator on his cell phone. Antawn and Theo were in the back. Their contribution was to curse every time Corey came close to hitting a car.

"We're going north, I mean south. South I mean to say, south. It's a black Nissan Sentra, license plate STN 967."

"Satan," Theo commented, "look out!"

"I saw him!" Corey said. "I asked him, what would he have done to me if I'd gotten in his way and he said, 'you don't want to know.' All this time he was getting his hooks into her...playing her like she was some—"

"I know I said north, but I meant south," Luke said. "Shut

up, Corey, you can get therapy later. Okay, he's turning onto Stirling Road, so Stirling and State Road Seven."

The traffic was thinner here and Corey could get closer. Renee was plastered against the back window of the car like a poster child for stranger danger. "Goddamn him!" Corey shouted. "I'll kill him if he hurts her."

Luke elbowed him to shut him up. "He's abducted a little girl and he was just arrested yesterday for bringing a gun— no, we're going west now, west!"

"Give me that phone!" Corey screamed.

"I don't know," Luke wailed into the phone. "Guys, what city are we in?"

"Pembroke Pines," Antawn said.

"No, I think it's Davie," said Theo.

"It could be the Indian Reservation," Luke said, "because—"

Corey grabbed the phone from him. "What is your problem? Are you worried about jurisdiction? This is my sister. This werewolf has my sister in the car and—"

That was all he got to say before Luke grabbed the phone back. "Are you sending help or just asking me questions?"

"Look out!" Antawn screamed.

"I've got it covered." Corey nearly went on two wheels to avoid sideswiping a light truck.

"You better calm down, man, you're gonna kill us," Theo said. "He can't hurt her as long as he's driving."

"He can if he drives into a pole!"

"Well, send the sheriff!" Luke said. "I know we're in Broward County—"

"Give me that," Corey made another grab but Luke held

on, and they struggled for it. The car swerved all over the road.

"God, please don't kill me before the playoffs," Antawn prayed.

The phone flew wild and hit the dash with a nasty, cracking sound. "Oh, no!" Corey pounded the wheel.

Luke tried it. "Dead. But she got all the information. How long can it take?..."

Noah turned south on Route 27. "No!" Corey wailed, pounding the wheel again. "No! No! No!"

"The cops'll find us anyway, the way you're driving!" Antawn said.

"You shouldn't be driving," Luke said. "Slide over."

Corey gripped the wheel harder. "No, it's fine. Oh, God, this is all my fault. I could have told her yesterday what happened. I couldn't put two and two together. What kind of idiot—"

Luke took the wheel and moved as if to sit right on Corey's lap. "Slide!"

The car swerved violently. "I can't see!" Corey yelled.

"Then move!"

Corey had to give in. "Don't let him get away!" he said, struggling into the passenger seat.

"I won't." Luke's driving, Corey had to admit, was much steadier. They were out in the country now and there was almost no traffic. Luke was gaining on him.

"She trusted him," Corey raved. "That creep! Who would do this to a little girl?"

"Let Corey drive again!" Antawn said to Luke. "It's better than having him talk!"

Luke was much closer to the Nissan than Corey had

been. Suddenly, Noah pulled onto the shoulder. So suddenly, in fact, that Luke shot past him and had to throw it in reverse. Noah was out of his car, reaching in and grabbing at Renee.

"Comeon-comeon-comeon!" Corey realized he was hitting Luke like a jockey would smack a horse to make it run.

Luke backed up and angled across Noah's car, making it almost impossible for Noah to get back out onto the road. Corey was impressed with that kind of thinking. They all piled out. Meanwhile Noah was dragging Renee up the embankment by the wrist. He had picked his area well. There was no one around. Corey saw something shiny flash in Noah's hand.

"Watch out, he's got a knife or something!" he yelled.

"Corey!" Renee screamed.

Noah stopped at the top of the hill. He was panting and grinning down at them. He held up his right hand, displaying a closed switchblade. "Don't come any closer," he said needlessly, because they had all stopped in their tracks. He pulled Renee in close to his body and held the knife just under her chin. The blade flicked open. Tears streamed down Renee's face.

"Let her go!" Corey shouted in a voice that came out thin and childish. "She didn't do anything to you!"

"We called the cops, Travers!" Luke said. "They're on their way."

"You're just adding to your charges, stupid!" Antawn hollered.

Noah laughed at them. "I don't care what happens to me now," he said. "My life is already screwed up. You see,

Brennan?" He gave Renee a shake. "You see what it feels like when somebody messes with the only thing you care about?"

Corey felt frozen, unable to speak. He felt like if he opened his mouth, horrible sounds would come out. Shakes ran up through his body in waves. Peripherally, he saw Luke edging closer to him.

"Let her go," Corey choked out the words, "or you won't have time to hurt her before I kill you."

This made Noah laugh—a happy, boyish laugh. Renee had detached, was staring off to the side, all the color drained out of her face. The pig had gotten grass stains on her dress, dragging her up that hill. It was a brand new dress.

Corey knew he had to think fast because his buddies were about to charge, and he knew that would make Noah hurt Renee.

"Noah!" he shouted. "Look at what you're doing!"

Noah laughed at him. The other guys were crouching, bouncing, waiting to move.

"Noah, I know you lied to me and lied to me. I know that now. But I believed you on one thing. About your parents and how they've cheated."

"Shut up, Corey!" Noah's face flushed.

"You went down the same road as them! Maybe you didn't mean to, but you did. You've been cheating since you got here. You're cheating now!"

"Shut UP!"

"But you didn't have to! Noah, you're a great player! If you'd just waited, you would have gotten everything you wanted without having to hurt anybody!"

"You stupid little—"

"Stop it now, Noah! Just stop, or else you're going to be the same as your mom and dad. Stop while there's still a little bit of a chance!"

Noah stood there, panting. Corey felt dizzy. The whole hillside seemed to be spinning.

Noah stared at Corey like he was seeing him for the first time. Something in his eyes seemed to flicker. His knife hand came down harmlessly at his side. Renee ran to Corey, slamming into him, crying. Sirens screamed in the distance.

Chapter

Corey waited in the parking lot of the Coral Way Mental Health Center. His parents and Renee's school counselors agreed she should have therapy twice a week while she was recovering from her trauma. Corey wondered at the time why nobody had suggested counseling for him, but it wasn't something he was willing to ask for. So he settled for

dropping her off and picking her up and trying to get as much vicarious insight as he could.

She was walking across the lot now in her long, black dress (this was something new) with her head down. Corey noticed her hands were clenched, not so much like angry fists, he thought, more like clenched with effort, like making this walk to the car was a hard job. Corey didn't think Renee had become depressed exactly, just very, very...careful. He wondered if there were any visible changes in him.

She slid into the passenger seat and slowly locked the seatbelt.

"How was it today?" Corey asked, firing the ignition.

"Not bad." She faced forward, like she had to help drive the car. "We talked about trust. Like, why did I trust Noah, but didn't trust you enough to tell you about it?"

"I did the same thing," Corey said, too eagerly, he thought. "Like, I didn't trust Luke enough to tell him about stuff Noah was doing."

"We both helped Noah succeed," she said.

"That's what your counselor says? It's our fault?"

She gathered her hair in her hands. "He said a lot of stuff, like, that I was just like Noah, in some ways. Noah doesn't have any trust, so he treats everybody like the enemy. He can't *discriminate,* was the word. And me, us I guess, can't either, so we tend to assume the best about people. Mr. Boyd says its better to be like us, because most people are okay, but once in a while, you meet a Noah, and wham!"

"What I figured out," Corey said eagerly, "is that I was sort of...stupid on purpose. I didn't listen to what my gut was telling me about Noah because that wasn't the story I wanted to hear."

"We need to grow up, Corey. We need to face the idea that there is bad in this world."

"Oh, I think I'm pretty well-convinced about that now!"

"But Mr. Boyd says I...we have to do that without going to the other extreme and becoming like Noah."

Corey sighed. "I like basketball. The bad guys wear a different color, so you always know what to do."

Renee laughed. It sounded so strange to Corey he wondered how long it had been since he'd heard her do it. "Mr. Boyd would *love* you!"

***

Deep breathing wasn't going to get it. Corey was never calm on the bench. This was *the* game—what they'd trained and sweated for since they were freshmen—what they'd risked everything for. The all-city trophy glowed on the scorekeeper's table. Fifteen inches of spun gold, depicting the all-mighty hoop—its delicate gold mesh net swirling to one side as a golden ball, trapped forever in time, swooshed through. They had all touched it before the game. Corey had felt its smooth goldness in his hands.

They were five minutes into the fourth quarter. At the end of the third, it was Coral Springs 31, St. Philip 42. Landis, acting like he thought it was an ordinary game, followed the rule book and pulled out Luke, Corey, and Theo to rest. Now it was five minutes later, and 38–46. Soon, Antawn would start to panic and miss shots, and the gap would close even more. Ricky was stone-cold. He couldn't even hit the rim. The second stringers were just in the way.

Corey jumped up and grabbed Landis's shoulder. "I'm rested!"

Landis was busy shouting at the court. He waved Corey off like a bug. "I know what I'm doing," he muttered.

"No, you don't!" Corey blurted and automatically stepped back.

Landis whirled and gave him laser-eyes. "Sit down or you won't even *see* the end of the game!"

Corey went and sat down. "I screwed that up," he said to Luke. "Now he'll make us wait even longer to show who's boss."

"We don't have much longer." Luke's whole body was jerking as he craned to follow the action.

Only Theo was calm. He had closed his eyes and bowed his head. Corey knew from experience that Theo was praying to the Baptist God.

Luke took out his medal. "Seems like a good idea," he said.

The scoreboard flashed 40–44. Corey was not impressed with the Baptist *or* Catholic Gods.

Landis tapped him. "Okay, next time-out, you three go in."

"Amen," Theo said quietly.

"Antawn!" Corey hissed. "Foul somebody!"

"Corey!" Landis barked. He lowered his voice. "You can pull a technical for something like that!"

But Antawn had heard his instructions. He grabbed the nearest jersey and held on, making a Coral Springs guard spin like a top. Whistles blew from every direction.

Relieved, Corey jogged out with the others. They lined up for the Coral Springs guy to take his shots. If he made both, it would be 42–44. There were six minutes on the clock. Corey could expand the lead comfortably if he didn't seize up or make stupid mistakes.

The Coral Springs guard was Ramon "Speedy" Gonzales. He was one of those guys who took the full ten seconds for his free throw: double dribbling, aiming, bouncing on the balls of his feet.

Bored, Corey looked at the crowd, much bigger than he was used to. They were in the Coral Springs Sports Complex, a cavernous gym with bad acoustics. Today the walls were strung with banners for Twix, which was sponsoring the event. All the sportswriters Corey knew were there, including Patti Starr, plus a camera crew from Channel Seven, which had extensively covered Noah's trial.

Corey watched Theo, whose game had been off ever since the trial. Corey could still remember how brave he looked in his blue suit, standing up and testifying, telling the truth about himself, risking everything because it was the right thing to do. Afterward, the reporters had descended on him like sharks. The most private person Corey had ever known was all over the newspapers. Two of the second string guys quit the team with no explanation, forcing them to rely on alternates. Nobody openly picked on Theo, but kids looked at him funny in the hallways, sometimes laughed when he walked past. Still, the important things hadn't changed. Duke sent Theo a letter calling him a hero and promising his scholarship was still there for him. And Antawn was working hard to pretend he wasn't having trouble with the situation. But all the hugging and patting that had gone on between them, Antawn was shying away from that so far.

Gonzales made his first shot: 41–44. Corey would insist on getting the ball, get two easy layups right away, and then maybe risk a three-pointer.

Speedy was setting up his second shot. *How did he get that nickname?* Corey looked for his family. Beth was absent, finally on her honeymoon. The wedding had been postponed until after the trial. Renee saw Corey looking and waved her arms over her head. She seemed better, although she still had nightmares.

Noah's sentence was two years in some kind of boot camp in Jacksonville. If he was black, Antawn had commented, he'd be in Stark, giving manicures to the axe murderers. It didn't seem like enough for all the trouble he'd caused. One day during the trial, Corey and Luke had been out in the corridor talking to Officer Gemelli, and she'd told them Noah's lust for revenge had done him in. Before he abducted Renee, they were planning to let him give information on where he'd bought his gun, and he could have walked free.

Gonzales missed his second shot. Knowing Antawn would get the ball, Corey pivoted and raced to the goal, positioning himself. Before Coral Springs could even set up a defense, Antawn had the ball to Corey, and Corey had it in the hole.

"All right!" Landis shrieked.

Theo blocked the next Coral Springs shot, but this time, Coral Springs was ready and put both guards on Corey. He could have passed to Luke but he didn't want to. Big guards didn't scare him like they used to. He'd learned you can charge right into a situation that scares you.

He pressed forward, making them both move out of his way, and put another one in. The score in his head was 41–48, but he wasn't sure anymore.

It seemed like everyone in the arena was screaming. The cheerleaders had abandoned their beautiful dance chants and were screeching, "Corey! Go!" Landis and the two Coral Springs coaches were yelling words Corey couldn't make out.

Coral Springs was running scared and emulated St. Philip's strategy of staying with their go-to guy. They rocketed downcourt and passed to Jeff Spurier, a master of the triple, so famous for closing gaps they called him Zipper. The Zipper was working well.

"Score?" Corey called to Landis as they ran by.

"Forty-one, forty-eight and three minutes!"

Corey tripped and went down. His whole body panicked and he jumped up listening for a whistle, but apparently he'd just tripped on his own feet. Meanwhile, Luke had missed a shot and the Zipper was back in his three-point zone, popping in another of his perfect triples: 44-48. The crowd went nuts.

How much time was left?

Antawn passed to Corey who missed. He knew his concentration was flagging. Luke tried for the rebound and missed. The team was panicking. Coral Springs picked up the rebound and took off.

"Get Spurier!" Corey screamed at his guards. But Theo was too slow and Spurier did it again: 47-48 and the Coral Springs fans were roaring.

Landis called a time-out. As they huddled around, raining sweat onto the floor, Landis spoke only to Corey. "Jeff Spurier looks like Noah, doesn't he? Tall, curly hair, likes to make those long shots? Did you notice?"

Corey smiled. It was all he needed.

The rest was a blur. The images were dreamlike. Corey felt like he was flying around the court with his feet not touching the ground. He remembered making a triple, but in his mind, it was like he had jumped in the air, over the guard's head, in some kind of slow motion. He guarded Spurier himself, blocking every shot. *You'll never get my trophy, Noah. You'll never get anything else that belongs to me.* The buzzer rang out on a final shot of Corey's that went in. He looked at the scoreboard and saw 47-53.

Corey's knees buckled. He went down on the floor and felt his teammates crash into and on top of him. Theo scooped him up and bear-hugged him. He went from hug to hug like a pinball: Ricky; Antawn, who grabbed his hand and jitterbugged; Landis, who almost crushed his ribs. Franny rushed forward and then stopped, not sure if her hug was welcome. Corey picked her up and twirled her. All was forgiven. They'd both been used by the same guy, after all. Claire and Luke had been standing in the center of the gym, glued together and swaying. Luke had tears streaming down his face, and Corey wondered if he was crying too. He knew he was when Luke reached out and pulled Corey in to hug them both. "Thank you," Luke whispered in his ear.

"And also with you," Corey managed to choke.

Another hand patted him, and he turned and found Jeff Spurier there, holding out his hand, returned to his real identity. "Nice game," he said. "I don't know what got into you at the end, but I looked in your eyes and I knew it was over."

Corey shook his hand. "Wish I had you on my team," he said.

Spurier laughed. "Me too!"

The last thing Corey saw before he was hoisted up in the air and carried around the gym by a bunch of strangers, was Antawn, throwing his arms around Theo.

***

The TV camera was disconcerting, like a big, staring eye. They were posed in the locker room: Corey sitting on the floor with his arms wrapped around the all-city trophy, his teammates clustered around him, Landis standing in the background near a carefully positioned Twix banner. The reporter was Angela St. Angelo, who had covered the trial and was putting this story in as a happy ending. The print reporters sat around waiting their turn.

"How did the trial affect you?" she asked, holding the mike so any of them could answer. "Did it take your focus off the game, or make it stronger?"

Corey answered. "We had to take time out from school to testify, so we were kind of worn out, but we always got in our extra practices and stuff. We wanted this really bad!"

The team made echoing sounds.

"Theo," she asked, "what about you? This trial forced you to make your sexual orientation public. What has the cost been to you?"

Corey saw Theo flinch a little, but they were all getting used to this.

"My friends and my coach have been very supportive," Theo recited. "If other people have had a problem with it, there's nothing I can do about that. I've got a full scholarship to Duke next year, and I'm looking forward to the future." His eyes were calm as he spoke, but Corey noticed he was sweating. Nobody really knew how easy or hard the future was going to be for him.

"How's your sister?" Angela asked Corey.

"She's fine, she came to the game today."

"Do you guys feel like heros?"

"Nah," Luke answered. "But we feel like really great basketball players."

She paused while they laughed again. "But seriously. You assisted in a police investigation, you risked your lives to save Corey's little sister, and you still managed to come out here today and win it all. That's pretty amazing. Do you know what it is, what makes you so special? Is there a secret you can pass down to younger players?"

Corey didn't know what to say. Landis stepped forward, crouched down and put his hand on Corey's shoulder. "They don't know because it's just who they are. But I know because I've coached a lot of teams before. I've had a few who loved to win just as much as these guys. They really love to win and that's important. But what I've never seen before, in any team I ever coached, is five guys who love each other this much."

Corey had to duck his head quickly, hoping the camera wouldn't catch his momentary lack of control. When he looked up again, he saw Patti Starr, tears running down her face, scribbling away.